THINGS
WE
KNOW
BY
HEART

Also by Jessi Kirby
Golden
In Honor
Moonglass

THINGS

WE

KNOW

BY

JESSI KIRBY

HARPER TEEN
An Imprint of HarperCollinsPublishers

HarperTeen is an imprint of HarperCollins Publishers.

Things We Know by Heart
Copyright © 2015 by Jessi Kirby
All rights reserved. Printed in the United States of America.
No part of this book may be used or reproduced in any manner whatsoever
without written permission except in the case of
brief quotations embodied in critical articles and reviews.
For information address HarperCollins Children's Books, a division
of HarperCollins Publishers, 195 Broadway, New York, NY 10007.
www.epicreads.com

Library of Congress Cataloging-in-Publication Data
Kirby, Jessi.
Things we know by heart / Jessi Kirby. — First edition.
pages cm
Summary: A year after losing her boyfriend, Trent, in an unexpected
accident, Quinn Sullivan secretly tracks down the recipient of his donated
heart in an attempt to heal, but ends up falling for him.
ISBN 978-0-06-229943-7 (hardcover)
[1. Grief—Fiction. 2. Love—Fiction. 3. Heart—Transplantation—Fiction.]
I. Title.
PZ7.K633522Th 2015   2014038649
[Fic]—dc23   CIP
                                                                        AC

Half title page illustration by Grace Lee
Typography by Erin Fitzsimmons
15 16 17 18 19   LP/RRDH   10 9 8 7 6 5 4 3 2 1

First Edition

For my sisters, whose hearts are brave and beautiful

heart (n):
a hollow muscular organ that pumps the blood through
the circulatory system by rhythmic contraction and
dilation;
the center of the total personality, especially with refer-
ence to intuition, feeling, or emotion
the central, innermost, or vital part of something
*   —definition of the word* heart

I DON'T KNOW how I knew, when the sirens woke me just before dawn, that they were for him.

I don't remember jumping out of bed, or tying the laces of my shoes. I don't remember my legs carrying me down the driveway, onto the winding stretch of road between our houses. I don't remember the feel of my feet hitting the ground, or my lungs taking in air, or my body racing to catch up with what I already knew in my heart was true.

But I remember every detail after that.

I can see the blue and red lights, swirling garishly against the pale sunrise sky. Hear the clipped voices of the medics. The words *head trauma* repeated over the loud jumble of their radios in the background.

I remember the deep, choking sobs of a woman I didn't

know and still don't, even now. The odd angle of her white SUV, its hood hidden by the broken stalks and scattered blooms of the sunflowers that grew along the side of the road. The fence, splintered and broken.

I remember glass like gravel, all over the asphalt.

Blood. Too much.

And his sneaker, lying on its side in the middle of it all. The heart I'd drawn in black Sharpie on the bottom.

I can still feel the emptiness of his shoe when I picked it up, and the way the absence of weight brought me to my knees. I can feel the strong grip of the gloved hands that lifted me and then held me back when I tried to run to him.

They wouldn't let me. Didn't want me to see him. And so what I remember most about that morning is standing on the side of the road, alone, darkness closing in around me as the day was unfolding. Morning sunlight on the vibrant gold petals, scattered where he lay dying.

"Communicating with the transplant recipients may help donor families in their grief. . . . Overall, donor families and recipients, as well as their relatives and friends, may benefit from exchanging thoughts and emotions about their experiences with donation . . . the gift of life. . . . It may take months and even years before someone is ready to send and/or receive correspondence, or you may never hear from them."
—*Life Alliance Donor Family Services Program*

CHAPTER ONE

FOUR HUNDRED DAYS.

I repeat the number in my head. Let it take over the hollow feeling as I grip the steering wheel. I can't let it go by like any other day without doing this. Four hundred deserves something, some sort of acknowledgment. Like 365, when I brought flowers to his mom but not to his grave because I knew he would've wanted her to have them. Or like his birthday, when it passed. That was four months, three weeks, and one day after. Day 142.

I'd spent it alone, because I couldn't handle seeing his parents that day, and because a tiny, secret part of me actually believed that if I was alone, then maybe somehow there was still a chance he could come back, turn eighteen, and pick up where we'd left off. Be a senior with me, apply to the same colleges, go to our last homecoming and prom, throw our caps into the sky at graduation and kiss in the sunshine before they hit the ground.

When he hadn't come back, I'd wrapped myself in the sweatshirt that still held the faintest hint of his smell, or maybe it was my imagination. I pulled it tight around me, and I made a wish. I wished, so hard, that I didn't have to do any of those things without him. And my wish came true. Senior year became a fog. I didn't mail my college applications. Didn't go dress shopping. Forgot there was even a sky or sunlight to kiss under.

The days passed, one after another, measured out in an unbroken, never-ending rhythm. Seemingly infinite, but gone in the blink of an eye—like waves crashing on the shore, or the seasons passing.

Or the beating of a heart.

Trent had an athlete's heart: strong, steady, ten beats slower than mine. Before, we'd lie there chest to chest, and I'd slow my breathing to match his, try to trick my pulse into doing the same; but it never worked. Even after three years, my pulse sped up just being near him. But we found our own synchronicity together, his heart thumping out a slow, steady beat and mine filling in the spaces between.

Four hundred days and too many heartbeats to count.

Four hundred days and too many places and moments where Trent no longer exists. And still no answer from one of the only places he does.

A horn blares from behind, yanking me from my thoughts and the nervous-sick feeling in my stomach. In the rearview mirror I can see the driver cursing as he swerves around me—angry hand raised in the air, lips spitting a question through his windshield: *What the hell are you doing?*

I asked myself the same thing when I got in the car. I'm not sure of *what* I'm doing, only that I have to do it because I have to see him for myself. Because of the way it felt to see the others.

Norah Walker was the first recipient to make contact with Trent's family, though they didn't learn her name until later. Recipients can reach out to the families of their donors at any time through the transplant coordinator and vice versa, but the letter still came as a surprise to us all. Trent's mom called the day after she got it and asked me to come over; and we sat there in the bright living room together, in the house that held so many memories, beginning with the day I'd run past it for the fifth time, hoping he'd notice me.

The sound of his footsteps trying to catch mine had slowed me down just enough to let them. His voice, unfamiliar to me then, worked to fit his words between breaths.

"Hey!"

Breath.

"Wait!"

Breath.

We were fourteen. Strangers until that moment. Until those two words.

As I sat in Trent's house with his mom, on the couch where he and I used to watch movies and eat popcorn out of the same bowl, it was a stranger's words, and the gratitude within them, that shook me out of the dark, lonely place I'd inhabited for so long. Her letter, written in a shaky hand on beautiful paper, lifted something in me that day. It was humble. Deeply sorry for Trent's death. Profoundly grateful for the life he'd given her.

I'd gone home that night and written her back, my own thank-you for the moment of lightness she'd granted me with her words. And the night after, I wrote to another recipient, and another—five in all. Anonymous letters to anonymous people I wanted to know. And when I sent them to the transplant coordinator to forward on, it was with the tenuous hope that those people would write me back. That they would notice me like he did.

I glance over my shoulder and he's there, smiling, gripping a sunflower that's taller than me, its stem trailing behind him, roots and all.

"I'm Trent," he says. "Just moved in back down the road a little

ways. You must live close, right? I've seen you run by every morn-
ing this week. You're fast."

I bite my bottom lip as we walk. Smile inside. Try not to confess
that I've saved my speed for the stretch of road in front of his house
every day since the moving truck pulled into the driveway and he
stepped out.

"I'm Quinn," I say.

Breath.

Writing the letters made me feel like I could breathe
again. I wrote about Trent and all the things he'd given me
when he was alive. The feeling I could do anything. Happiness. Love. The letters were a way to honor him, and a hope
for something more. An anonymous hand reaching out into
the emptiness, looking for a connection. An answer.

I laugh, because he's still out of breath, and because he doesn't
seem to remember the giant sunflower dangling from his hand.

"Oh," he says, following my glance, "this was supposed to be
for you. I . . ." He runs a nervous hand through his hair. "I, um,
I got it over there, near that fence."

He holds it out to me and laughs. It's a sound I want to keep
hearing.

"Thank you," I answer. And I reach out to take it. The first
thing he ever gave me.

I got four answers from the people he gave to.

After 282 days, multiple letters back and forth, consent
forms, and premeeting counseling, his mom and I drove

to the Donor Family Services office together and sat side by side as we waited for them to arrive. To meet them face-to-face.

Just as Norah had been the first to reach out with words, she was the first to reach out her hand, and in spite of all the times I'd imagined meeting her, nothing could've prepared me for the way it made me feel to take that hand in mine, and to look in her eyes and know that there was a part of Trent there too. A part that had saved her life and given her a chance to be a mother to the curly-haired little girl who peeked out from behind her legs and a wife to the man who stood crying beside her.

When she took a deep breath with Trent's lungs and brought my hand to her chest so I could feel them fill and expand, my heart filled right along with them.

It was the same with the others I met—Luke Palmer, seven years older than me, who played us a song on his guitar, and who could do that now because Trent had given him a kidney. There was John Williamson, a quiet but warm man in his fifties, who wrote beautifully poetic letters about how his life had changed since receiving his liver transplant but who fumbled to find the right words to speak to us in that little reception room. And then there was Ingrid Stone, a woman with pale-blue eyes so different from Trent's brown ones but who could see the world again, and paint it in vibrant colors on her canvases, because of them.

They say time heals all wounds, but meeting those people that afternoon—a makeshift family of strangers brought together by one person—healed more in me than all the time that passed in the days that had come before.

It's why, when day after day went by with no reply from the last recipient, I started looking for him. It's the reason I searched—matched up dates with news stories and hospitals—until I found him so easily, I almost didn't trust it. It's also why, around anyone else, I've pretended like I understand the reasons he hasn't responded. That, like the woman at Donor Family Services told us, some people never do, and that's their choice.

I've acted like I don't think about him every day and wonder about that choice. Like I've made peace with it. But alone, in those endless hours that stretch to eternity before the morning, I always come back to the truth: that I haven't at all. And I don't know if I can unless I do this.

I don't know what Trent would think if he knew. What he would say if he could somehow see. But it's been four hundred days. I hope he would understand. For so long, *I* was the one with his heart. I just need to see where it is now.

"The heart has its reasons, of which reason knows nothing: we know this in countless ways."

—*Blaise Pascal*

CHAPTER TWO

THERE ISN'T A place to turn around on this road, even if I wanted to. Just a steep drop down a hillside of moss-covered oak trees that rise up out of the tall, summer-gold grass. The road goes on for miles like that, winding its way all the way to the coast, where he's been all nineteen years of his life. Thirty-six miles away.

When the trees finally give way to the wide blue expanse of ocean and sky at the edge of his town, my hands are shaking so badly, I have to pull into the scenic overlook on the shoulder of the highway. A thin swath of fog clings to the cliff's edge, melting beneath the morning sunlight that spreads over the water beyond. I turn off the car but don't get out. Instead I roll down the windows and breathe. Slow, deep breaths in an attempt to calm my conscience.

I've been here, to Shelter Cove, lots of times before. Driven past this spot and headed into the little beach town on countless spring and summer days, but today feels different.

There's none of the giddy anticipation that used to bubble between me and my sister, Ryan, in the backseat as we drove over with Mom and Dad, our trunk packed full of beach towels and boogie boards, cooler bursting with all the junk food we were never allowed to eat at home. There's no thrill of freedom that came when Trent first got his license and we'd drive over in his truck for the day, feeling grown-up and romantic. Today there's just a grim sort of determination, and the tense feeling that comes along with it.

I look out over the water, and a startling thought occurs to me. I wonder if, any of those times I've been here, I ever saw Colton Thomas. If Trent and I ever walked past him on the street, eyes catching for half a second before moving on without another thought, the way strangers do. Completely unaware that one day there would be this link between us. Before everything. Before Trent's accident, and writing letters, and meeting the others, and before I spent so many nights hoping to hear back from Colton Thomas and wondering why I never did.

It's a small town. Small enough that we could've seen each other at some point on one of my trips over. But then again, maybe not. He probably didn't spend his summers the way the rest of us did. I've studied the careful time line his sister kept on her blog, which is what eventually led me to him. Though she didn't start it until he was put on the transplant list, I know that he was fourteen when his heart began the excruciatingly slow process of failing him. He made the transplant list by the time he was seventeen. And he would've died had he not gotten the call in the eleventh hour of his eighteenth year. On the last day of Trent's seventeenth.

I push away the thought and the heavy feeling that comes along with it. Take another deep breath and remind myself how careful I need to be with this. I've broken too many rules already, written and unwritten, protocols meant to protect both the donor families and the recipients from knowing too much. Or expecting too much.

But when I found Colton, and his whole story out there for anyone to see, I replaced those rules in my mind with a new set. Rules and promises that I've repeated over and over, that have gotten me this far today and that bolster me enough to pull back onto the road as I repeat them: I will respect Colton Thomas's wish for no contact, though I don't think I'll ever understand it. I just want to *see* him. See who he is in reality. Maybe then I can understand. Or at least make peace with it.

I won't interfere with his life. I won't talk to him, not even to hear the sound of his voice. He won't even know I exist.

I park across the street from Good Clean Fun and shut off my car, but I don't get out. Instead I take a moment to absorb the details of the shop, like maybe I'll see something that can tell me more about Colton than all his sister's posts have. It looks just like it did in the pictures I've seen: perfectly stacked paddleboards and kayaks fill the racks on either side of the door, bright splashes of yellow and red against the otherwise gray morning. Behind them I can see through the front window, where an assortment of wet suits and life jackets hangs in neat rows, ready for the day's adventure-seeking customers. Nothing beyond what I was expecting. Even so, it's strange to see it now, a shop I must've walked by more than once and never paid any attention to. Today it's a place I feel like I know, with a history made up of so much more than the equipment on the racks.

The shop's not open yet, and the street is mostly empty; but up ahead, where the pier juts out into the choppy gray ocean, the locals are out, beginning their days. Surfers dot the water on either side of the mussel-covered supports. A fisherman baits his line before he casts over the railing. Two older ladies in tracksuits walk at a brisk pace along the water, chatting and pumping their arms enthusiastically as they go. And in the parking lot next to the pier, three guys in board shorts and flip-flops lean against the railing, watching the waves as steam curls lazily from the coffee cups in their hands.

I decide coffee might be a good idea. If nothing else, I could use a cup to hold in my own hands. Maybe that would be enough to steady them. And finding some would give me something to do besides sit across the street from the shop waiting, and becoming less and less sure of myself by the second.

A few doors down on my side of the street is a sign that looks promising: THE SECRET SPOT. I give the closed rental shop one more quick glance, then get out of the car and head down the sidewalk, trying to look comfortable and relaxed, like I belong here.

The air is thick with morning fog and the salt smell of the water, and though the day will heat up, it's still cool enough that goose bumps rise on my arms as I walk. When I push through the door of the café, the smell of coffee wraps around me, along with the mellow notes of acoustic guitar that come from the small speaker over the door. My shoulders relax the tiniest bit. I almost feel like if I wanted to, I could just get a coffee, maybe take a walk on the beach, and leave without crossing any more lines. But I know it's not true. There's too much wrapped up in this, and in him, for me to be able to do that.

I startle at the voice that comes from behind the counter.

"Morning! Be right with you." The voice is warm. Easy, like a smile.

"Okay," I answer, aware of how stiff I sound in contrast. Like I'm out of practice interacting with people. I try briefly to think of something else to add but come up blank. I step back and look around the café instead. It's a cozy place, with deep-turquoise walls that make the black-and-white surf photos on them stand out. Above me, colorful old surfboards hang side by side, suspended from the ceiling by loops of weathered rope. Next to the counter another surfboard—this one with a jagged bite taken out of it—leans against the wall, serving as the hand-painted menu board.

I'm not hungry at all, but I scan it anyway, looking for a breakfast burrito out of habit. Trent's favorite, especially after morning swim practice. If he got out early, and we had time before school, we'd go downtown and grab one to share at our own little secret spot: a bench hidden away behind the restaurant, overlooking the creek. Sometimes we'd talk—about his next meet or mine, or our plans for the weekend. But my favorite times were the ones when we'd just sit there with the soft sound of water flowing over rocks and the comfortable quiet that comes with knowing each other by heart.

A guy with wild blond hair and bright-blue eyes steps through the doorway from the kitchen, drying his hands on a towel. "Sorry about the wait," he says, flashing me a smile that shines white against his tan. "Help hasn't showed up yet. No idea why." He nods at the chalkboard reporting the day's surf conditions: *6 ft south swell, offshore breeze . . . get out there!*

When he glances out the window toward the beach and

shrugs, I get the idea he's okay with it.

I don't say anything. Pretend to examine the menu. The silence is a little awkward.

"Anyway," he says, clapping his hands together, "what can I get you this mornin'?"

I don't really want anything, but I'm here, and it feels too late to duck out now. Plus he seems nice. "I'll have a mocha," I say, not sounding entirely sure.

"That's it?" he asks.

I nod. "Yes."

"You sure you don't want anything else?"

"Yes. I mean no thank you—I'm sure." My eyes drop to the ground, though I can feel him looking at me.

"Okay," he says after a long moment. His voice gentler now. "I'll bring it over to you in just a minute." He gestures at the five or six empty tables. "Plenty of seats—take your pick."

I do, a table tucked deep in the corner, facing the window. Outside, the sun melts its way through the morning gray, infusing the water with light and color.

"Here you go."

The café guy sets down a steaming, bowl-sized mug and a plate with a giant muffin. "Banana chocolate chip," he says when I look up. "Tastes like happiness. You seem like maybe you could use a little this morning, so it's on the house. The coffee, too."

He smiles, and I recognize the careful way he does it. It's not just this morning. It's the same smile people have given me for a while now, a mix of what looks like compassion and pity, and I wonder what it is he sees in me that makes him think I need it. My posture? Expression? Tone? It's hard to guess after this long.

"Thank you," I say. And then I try for a real smile back, to assure both of us that I'm okay.

"See? It's working already." He grins. "I'm Chris, by the way. Let me know if you need anything else, okay?"

I nod. "Thank you."

He goes back to the kitchen, and I lean back in my chair, hot mug cradled between my hands, feeling a little calmer already. Though I can still see the kayak shop across the street, this feels like a safe, reasonable distance. Like I haven't done anything wrong by being here. A surfer walks by on the sidewalk, and I catch a glimpse of green eyes and tan skin that sends my eyes away quickly, down toward the foam of my mocha. He's striking. It's startling to notice, and doing so doesn't come without a twinge of guilt.

A moment later the door swings open, and he strides straight toward the counter without seeing me in my corner, dings the bell five times fast. "Hey! Anybody working here today, or you all out in the water?"

Chris comes back from the kitchen, a smile of familiarity on his face. "Well, look who decided to grace us with his presence this morning." They high-five and pull each other into one of those guy half-hugs over the counter. "Good to see you, man. You surf already?"

"Watched the sun come up from the water," says the one with those eyes. "Just came in. It was good—why didn't I see you out there?" He reaches for a cup and fills it himself.

"Somebody's gotta run the place," Chris says, taking a sip from his own cup.

"Somebody's priorities are all wrong," the other one deadpans.

Chris sighs. "It happens."

"I know. When you're not looking," his friend says simply. He blows gently over his cup. "That's why you gotta be here now, so you don't miss that stuff."

"That's deep, dude." Chris smiles. "Any more wisdom you want to lay on me this morning?"

"Nope. But this swell's supposed to hold up. Sunrise session tomorrow?"

Chris tilts his head, reordering his priorities.

"Come on." His friend smiles. "Life's too short. Why would you *not*?"

"All right," Chris says. "You're right. Five thirty. You want grub?"

When a tiny part of me hopes he answers yes so he'll stay, I realize how intently I've been following their conversation. And him. Self-conscious, I raise my mug to my lips, more to have something to hide behind than to take a sip. I force my eyes back to the street outside the window.

"Nah, I gotta go get the shop opened up. I got a family of eight coming in to rent kayaks right now, and I promised my sister I'd be there to get 'em set up."

His words, casually spoken, hit me quick, like a volley of arrows: *kayaks, rental shop, sister.* My stomach does a flip at the all-too-real possibility that this is *him*. Standing right there, just a few feet away. I inhale sharply at the thought and immediately choke on my coffee. Both guys look my way as I sputter and reach for the glass of water on the table. I knock over my mug instead, sending it to the ground with a crash. Coffee splatters in every direction.

The surfer takes a step toward me as I jump up, out of my seat. Chris tosses a rag over the counter to him. "Colt, catch."

My heart drops right out of my chest, taking all the air in the room with it so I can't breathe.

Colt.

As in Colton Thomas.

"Scientists have identified individual neurons, which fire, when a particular person has been recognized. Thus, [it is possible that] when a recipient's brain analyzes the features of a person, who significantly impressed the donor, the donated organ may feed back powerful emotional messages, which signal recognition of the individual. Such feedback messages occur within milliseconds and the recipient [may even believe] that [he] knows the person."

—*"Cellular Memory in Organ Transplants"*

CHAPTER THREE

COLTON THOMAS WALKS over to me, dark brows creased with concern, rag in one hand, the other reaching across the puddle of spilled coffee. "You okay?"

I nod, still coughing, though I'm far from it.

"Here, step over this way. I'll get it." He takes my elbow lightly, and I tense at his touch.

"Sorry," he says, dropping his hand quickly. "I . . . you sure you're okay?"

He's standing there, right there in front of me with a dishrag in his hand. Asking me if I'm okay. This should not be happening. This isn't what was supposed to happen, this—

I look away. Cough once more, then clear my throat and take a shaky breath in. *Calm down, calm down.* "I'm sorry," I manage. "So sorry. I just . . ."

"It's okay," he says, like he might laugh. He glances over his shoulder at Chris, who looks like he's already making me a new cup.

"Fresh one on the way!" Chris calls.

"See?" Colton Thomas says. "No worries." He gestures at the closest chair. "I got this. You can sit."

I don't move, and I don't say anything.

He crouches down to sop up the coffee with the rag but then looks back up at me and smiles, and it shocks me because of how different this smile is from the weak one in so many of his sister's pictures. Because *he* doesn't look like he did in the pictures. I don't think I would've guessed he was even the same person. Maybe not even if he'd walked right into his parents' shop.

The Colton in the pictures was ill. Pale skin, dark circles, puffy face, thin arms. A smile that seemed to take effort. This person kneeling down in front of me is vibrant, and healthy, and the one who—

I want to look away, but I can't. Not with the way he looks at *me* then.

His hand stills and hovers above the sticky floor like he's

forgotten what he's doing. And then, without taking his eyes off me, he stands slowly until we're face-to-face and I can see the deep green of his eyes as they search mine.

His voice is softer, almost tentative, when he finally speaks. "Are you . . . have you . . . do I?"

His questions float, unasked, in the space between us, and for moment they hold me there. And then panic comes rushing in.

The reality of what I've done—or come dangerously close to doing—hits me, sends me past him with a bump to his shoulder and out the door before he can say anything else. Before we can look at each other a moment longer.

I don't look back. I walk as fast as I can down the sidewalk to my car, driven by the certainty that I shouldn't have come and that I need to leave *now*. Because mixed up with the knowledge that I've done something horribly wrong is the overwhelming feeling that I want to know this person better. Colton Thomas, with green eyes and tan skin, and a smile like he knows me. Who seems so different from the person I thought I'd find.

The sound of the door behind me, and then footsteps, makes me want to run.

"Hey," a voice calls. "Wait!" His voice.

Those two words.

They make me want to—stop and wait, turn, and just look at him again. But I don't. I walk faster instead. Away.

This was a mistake, a mistake, a mistake. I jam my hand into my pocket and click the unlock button on my key over and over, near frantic now. Just as I step off the sidewalk and reach for my door, his footsteps come right up behind me, close.

"Hey," he says again, "you left this."

I freeze, fingers curled tight under the handle.

My heart hammers as I turn, slowly, to face him again.

He swallows hard. Holds my purse out to me. "Here."

I take it. "Thank you."

We stand there, catching our breaths. Searching for more words. He finds his first.

"I . . . are you all right? You seem like . . . maybe you're not?"

Tears well up instantly, and I shake my head.

"I'm sorry," he says, taking a step back. "That was—it's none of my business. I just . . ." His eyes run over my face, searching again.

This is more than a mistake. I yank up on the handle and swing the door open, duck inside, and close it behind me with a shaky hand. I need to leave right now. I fumble with my keys for the right one, but they all look the same, and I can feel his eyes on me, and I just need to leave, and I should never have come, and— I find the right key, jam it into the ignition, and turn it. When I do, I look up in time to see him take a startled step out of the way, back onto the

23

sidewalk. I shove the gear into drive, turn the wheel, and hit the gas. Hard.

The impact is sudden and loud. An insult that comes out of nowhere. Metal and glass crunch. My chin smacks into the steering wheel. The horn blares, and in the stillness of the moment it sinks in, what I've just done. Everything I've just done. I close my eyes, hoping feebly that somehow none of it happened. That I just dreamed it, the way I dream about Trent, where everything is so clear and real, until I wake up and realize that I am alone and he is gone.

Slowly, I open my eyes. I'm afraid to do anything else, but my hand moves automatically, puts the car in park. And then my door swings open.

Colton Thomas is not gone. He's right there, looking at me with concern and something else I'm not sure of. He leans in and reaches across me to shut the engine off.

"Are you okay?" There's worry in his voice.

My mouth throbs, but I nod my head, avoid his eyes, bite back tears. I taste blood.

"You're hurt," he says.

He raises his hand, just barely, like he might brush the hair away from my face, or wipe the blood from my lip, but he doesn't. He just keeps looking at me.

"Please," he says after a long moment, "let me help."

"The heart, [scientists have found], is not just a pump but also an organ of great intelligence, with its own nervous system, decision-making powers, and connections to the brain. They found that the heart actually 'talks' with the brain, communicating with it in ways that affect how we perceive and react to the world."
—Dr. Mimi Guarneri, The Heart Speaks:
A Cardiologist Reveals the Secret
Language of Healing

CHAPTER FOUR

COLTON STANDS BETWEEN the bumper of my car and the blue VW bus's I ran into, taking in the damage. "It's really not that bad," he says, squatting down between the two bumpers. "I mean, *you* took the brunt of it." He looks at the clump of napkins I'm holding tight to my bottom lip. "That's gonna need stitches. We should get you to a doctor."

I try to ignore the "we" part. I need to get out of here even more than I did before, but I've just complicated things exponentially. "I can't just leave," I say. "I ran into someone's car. I have to make a report or something. Or at least call my insurance company. And my parents. Oh god." They were already gone when I left this morning and will probably expect me to be there when they came home for lunch, because I have been there every day for the last few weeks, since graduation.

Colton stands. "You can do all that later—you need to get yourself taken care of first. Just write a note. Leave your number. People are mellow around here. And you barely dented it. It's really not that big of a deal."

I want to argue with him, but my lip throbs, and the warm stickiness of the napkins I've got pressed to it is making me queasy. "Really?"

"Really," he says, glancing over his shoulder. "Hang on. I'll be right back."

He turns and jogs easily across the street to the kayak rental shop, where a small crowd—presumably the family he mentioned in the café—mills around. The adults alternately eye their watches and glance around while a couple of teenagers lean against the window, absorbed in their phones, and the two youngest kids chase each other between the racks of kayaks. I should go right now. Leave a quick note on the bus and get out of here now, before this goes any further.

I hurry back to my car and duck into the driver's seat to grab my purse. The sudden movement causes a whole new wave of pain and stickiness to rush to my mouth, and I have to take a deep breath before I dig through my purse for a pen and something to write on.

I look across the street, watch as Colton approaches the family of customers. He looks apologetic as he gestures back in my direction, likely explaining what just happened. They nod, and he takes out his phone, makes a brief call, then shakes everyone's hand again before turning to come back. I pretend to be so deeply absorbed in writing my note that I don't look up when his feet stop right in front of me.

"I can take you to the hospital," he says.

I write my name and phone number at the bottom of the note. "Thank you, really, but it's okay. I can drive myself."

"I don't know," he says. "You sure that's a good idea?"

"It's not that bad. I'm fine, I—"

"Here." He takes the slip of paper from me. Glances down at it. "Why don't I go put this on the car, you switch seats, and I can drive you."

I don't move. Partly because I know this is a bad idea and partly because I'm a little dizzy.

Colton crouches in front of me so I can't avoid his eyes. "Listen. You need stitches, I just got the day off work, and I can't let you just drive away like that."

He doesn't wait for me to answer but walks to the windshield of the bus, lifts the wiper, and tucks the note beneath it. Before I can come up with an excuse for him not to take me, he's back at the driver's side of my car, where I'm still sitting.

I look at him a moment longer, long enough to run through all the reasons that letting this go one step further is a mistake.

"Can I?" he asks. And when he looks at me with those eyes, something deep within them makes me say yes.

We don't speak as he drives down the main street, not at first. The sleepy little beach town has come to life now, and beachgoers crowd the sidewalks, heading down to the sand in their flip-flops and cover-ups, stuffed beach bags slung over their shoulders. I can feel him looking over at me every few seconds, and it takes all my focus not to make eye contact. Finally, when it seems like he's drifted into his own thoughts, I glance at him out of the corner of my eye, try to take in the details. Blue board shorts, white T-shirt, flip-flops. No MedicAlert bracelet. All this surprises me, like there should be some outward sign.

He seems comfortable driving my car, and I try to be okay with it, but I'm not. I don't think anyone else has driven it since Trent's been gone, and it feels like if I closed my eyes right now, I could see him there. Sitting in that seat, with one hand on the wheel, the other on my knee, singing loud with the radio and getting the words wrong on purpose to make me laugh. Working my name into every song that came on.

But there is no music on now, and Colton Thomas is

driving my car. A deep river of guilt runs through me, and as we drive, I try to come up with a new set of rules to deal with the situation I've created. I won't ask him any questions, and I'll answer as few as possible. I won't mention where I'm from, or why I was in Shelter Cove, or who I am. Maybe I won't even tell him my real name because—

"So, Quinn," he says, keeping his eyes on the road. "Let's start over."

I look at him now, startled at my own name. Then I remember the note I just signed.

"I'm Colton," he offers.

"I know." It slips out before I can stop it.

"You do?" There's a note of disappointment in his voice, one I don't understand.

I nod. Swallow. Wish I were anywhere but here. "Yeah," I say, too quickly. "I . . . you . . . your friend in the café said your name."

I glance at him to see if he believes me, then realize he has no reason not to. He has no idea what I know. A wave of nausea—or guilt, it's hard to say which—passes over me. I should just tell him the truth right now. Maybe he'd be so horrified he'd turn around and drive right back to his shop and get out, and that would be the end of it. I could leave and make sure our paths never crossed again. Close the door I shouldn't have opened. I open my mouth to say the words, but they catch and collide in the back of my throat.

"So you were listening?" Colton asks, with a hint of a smile. "Enough to catch my name?"

I look straight out the windshield and tell the truth. "I was."

"And you're not from here?"

"I'm not."

"You on vacation?"

I shake my head. "Just here for the day." I don't say from where.

"Alone?" His voice sounds hopeful.

"Yes."

We stop at a red light. He's quiet a moment, and I turn the word over in my mind. *Alone.* I've felt that way for so long. For four hundred days. Since the day Trent died, I've been alone *and* lonely. But right now, in this moment, I realize I'm not either one of those things.

I've imagined what it might be like to see Colton Thomas, wondered how it would feel to look from a distance at the person who received such a vital part of who Trent was. To look at a stranger's chest and know what lies deep within it. Trent's mom told me his grandmother was beside herself when she heard they had donated his heart. She didn't take issue with any of the other organs, but the heart was different. The heart was everything that made a person who he was, and she thought he should've been buried with it. I hoped, after meeting the others, that seeing another person who was alive because of Trent would be a healing thing. The *final* healing thing. But I didn't, at any of those times, imagine that when I did, I would somehow immediately feel less alone.

"That's not a bad start," Colton says, like he can hear my thoughts.

"Not a bad start for what?"

"A do-over," he says simply.

"The Greeks believed the spirit resided in the heart. In traditional Chinese medicine, the heart is believed to store the spirit, shen. *The idea of the heart as an inner book, which contains a record of a person's entire life—emotions, ideas, and memories—appears in early Christian theology, but may have ancient roots that go back to Egyptian culture.*

"No other part of the human body has been so widely commemorated in poetry, so commonly used as a symbol for love and the soul."

—Dr. Mimi Guarneri, The Heart Speaks:
A Cardiologist Reveals the Secret
Language of Healing

CHAPTER FIVE

WE BOTH TENSE when the ER doors swish open, and as soon as we step through the doorway, it brings me back to reality. Colton's reality, which, according to all his sister's posts, was lived in and out of hospitals, with endless medications in constant need of adjustment, extended stays, and emergency trips—scares that drove him and his family through these same doors fearing the worst. The thought of it makes me want to take his hand in mine as we walk up to the check-in counter.

Behind it, a round woman in mint-green scrubs sits in front of a computer, clacking away at the keys. We stand there for a moment before she looks up and runs her eyes disinterestedly over my face. They land, for a brief second, on the bloodied napkins I've got wadded at my lip; then she grabs a clipboard from her organizer and slides it across the counter for me before turning back to her computer.

"Have a seat and fill those out," she says without looking back at me. "We'll be with you as soon as we can."

Her voice is monotone, like she's said those words a million times, and it makes me wonder what would have to come through the doorway for her *not* to sound that way. But I don't have to wonder for long. "Thank you," I say, and she looks up again, but this time she catches sight of Colton and does a double take.

"*Colton*, honey! I'm so sorry; I didn't see you there!" She bolts up out of her chair and pushes through the door next to the counter, her hand on his arm in an instant. "Is everything okay? You need me to page Dr. Wilde?"

"No, no, I'm fine," he says. "I'm great, in fact. It's my friend here who needs to be seen. She's got a pretty good cut on her lip. I think it needs a few stitches."

The nurse puts a hand to her chest, visibly relieved. "Oh good." She looks at me apologetically. "I'm sorry—I don't mean good that *you're* hurt, just that Colton here—"

"Used to be kind of a regular," he cuts in. "I'm sorry; it was rude of me not to make any introductions." He smiles tightly at me and gestures to the nurse. "Quinn, this is Mary. Mary, my friend Quinn."

Mary holds his eyes for a moment before she looks at me again. Long enough for something—a question maybe, or an opinion—to pass between them. It makes me straighten my shoulders when she turns her attention back to me. "Well, Quinn, it's a pleasure to meet any friend of Colton's." She extends a petite but firm hand to me.

"It's nice to meet you too," I say, shaking it.

"So have you two known each other long?" she asks, my hand still in hers, still shaking.

I look at Colton.

"We just met," he says with a quick smile.

I nod, and the moment when it seems like he or I should explain further stretches tight between the three of us standing there, with Mary still holding my hand in both of hers.

Colton clears his throat, then gestures at the clipboard in my hand. "Why don't we go sit so you can get those filled out?"

"Yes, yes," Mary says, finally releasing my hand. "You two go and sit down, and as soon as you're finished, we'll take you back to a room." She smiles kindly at me, and it feels like an approval of sorts, one I'm sure I don't deserve.

"Thank you," I say again, and we turn to find a seat, but Mary's voice spins us right back around.

"Colton, honey," she says, looking at him with moist eyes. "You look so good; you really do." She shakes her head, and her eyes fill. "I can't believe it's been over a year now. It's just so good to see you so . . ." She steps into him and hugs him tight to her before he can do anything else.

It takes him a second, but he puts his arms around her in a hug that's awkward and tender at the same time. "It's good to see you too," he says.

Watching this moment feels like an intrusion when he so obviously was trying to avoid the subject. I turn and scan the room for a seat. There are only three other people in the ER waiting room: a guy slumped in his blue plastic chair like he's been there for far too long, cradling his arm in his lap, and an elderly couple sitting quietly side by side, each reading a different section of the paper. The man rests a hand on the woman's knee, a gesture that is so familiar and so clearly second nature for them both that it stops me where I stand. I can't remember the last time Trent rested his hand on my leg like that. But I do remember that every time he did, his fingers drummed like it was impossible for them to be still.

Colton's voice brings me back to the present. "Hey. Sorry about that."

I pull my eyes away from the couple as he sits down next

to me and exhales roughly.

"It's okay; she was nice—once she saw you." He looks at me and tries for a smile, but I can feel tension in it. "Anyway," I add, trying to lighten it, "seems like you might be a good person to know around here."

It's not a question, but it leaves room for a response. For an answer, if he wants to give one.

He doesn't. Just gives another tight smile and a nod and sits back in his chair, arms crossed over his chest. And just like that he's a million miles away next to me in his blue chair, and I am alone again. I search for something else to say, something that will change the subject, maybe even make him laugh, but I don't know what to say because, well, I don't know *him*.

So I don't say anything. I pick up the pen at the end of the little chain and start the forms. It's probably better anyway, this distance. Better that we don't go beyond this. I fill out the forms in silence while Colton sits next to me, feet absently tapping the floor, fingers thrumming on the arm of the chair, and in those moments we exist in separate universes, like we did before I came here and they collided.

"You don't have to stay here with me," I say when I finish with the last one. "I mean, if you want to go, it's okay. I'll be okay. You've done enough by getting me here, really."

This snaps him back from wherever he was. "What? No.

Why would I go anywhere?" He shifts in his chair so he's facing me, and his jaw softens. "I'm sorry. I really don't like hospitals, is all. Spent too much time in them already."

He pauses, like he knows he's left himself open for me to ask why. I can feel how much he doesn't want me to, and it's the last thing I want to talk about right now, so I don't ask. Questions are dangerous territory for us, and somehow we both seem to recognize this.

He offers an explanation anyway. "Accident-prone," he says. "Like you," he adds with a smile.

I see the whole sequence of events: me knocking over the coffee, running out of the café, crashing my car. And it makes me laugh—how it all must've looked to him. "I was pretty ridiculous back there, wasn't I?"

"No." Colton tries to keep a straight face as he shakes his head. "Not at all." He shrugs. Cracks a smile. "It was nothing. Nobody saw."

"*You* saw. And I was a total mess."

Colton laughs now too. "No, you just seemed . . ."

"Crazy. I seemed totally crazy. I'm sorry. This whole thing is really embarrassing."

"Not crazy," he says. "A little dangerous, maybe." He smiles again. "It's okay, though. I've done worse in front of people."

He looks at his lap, and the smile falters the tiniest bit. "I passed out once, in front of my whole class, in eighth grade.

Traumatized them all when I hit a desk on the way down and ended up having to get twelve stitches in my head. I had to walk around looking like a bald Frankenstein for a while after that." He laughs again, but it fades quickly.

We're quiet a moment, and it hits me square in the chest. This story is familiar. His sister wrote about it—how nobody realized at first why things like that had started to happen to him. And then those things started to get worse, almost overnight.

"Anyway," he says, turning to face me, "what you did was much more impressive."

"That's one way to put it." I look down, try to focus on the forms in my lap instead of how close we're sitting, but my eyes find their way back up to his. "Thank you for bringing me here. I'm pretty sure most people would've been scared off by that."

"I'm not most people," he says with a shrug. "And like I said, I was impressed." He clears his throat and glances at the counter. "So go ahead, give those to Mary. I'm not going anywhere."

As soon as I hand Mary the clipboard, another nurse in mint-green scrubs with wild, curly hair dyed bright red escorts me down the hall to an examination room. I sit on the thin, crinkly paper that covers the table and lower the hand that's been holding the napkins to my lip for what feels like forever. It seems like a good sign that I don't feel anything warm or sticky when I take them away, but I feel nervous all of a sudden. Exposed.

The nurse peers at my lip from where she stands, then puts a hand on either side of my head and tilts it back gingerly into the light to get a better view. "So you're a new friend of Colton's?" she asks, almost matter-of-factly. There's that same thing in her voice that was in Mary's. Interest. A trace of protectiveness.

"Um . . . yes." I don't know what answer is the right one, or if there is a right one at all. I open my mouth to explain, but the movement pulls at the cut on my lip and I wince a little instead.

She tilts my head back down so our eyes are level. "He is such a sweet boy. We just love him around here." She stands, moves to the counter, and comes back with a small stack of gauze pads and a bottle of rust-colored solution. "Lie right back there on the table for me, honey."

I obey, and she squirts some of the liquid onto the gauze, dabs gently at the skin around the cut. "He's been through so much, but he's a fighter, that one. Took it all on with more grace and courage than most people, you know?"

I nod like I do know, and she pushes off the floor with one foot, sending her stool to the trash can, steps on the pedal to flip open the top, and tosses in the soiled gauze pad. Then she slides back and squirts more solution onto a fresh piece of gauze, again dabbing at my lip, only now, closer to the actual cut. I flinch when she touches it directly.

"Sorry. It's tender, I know." She goes back to dabbing the edges. "The good news is it's small. Two or three stitches should do it. We'll get you fixed up and out of here in no time."

"Okay." I nod again, trying to stay calm, even though a quiet panic starts to rise in me. I've never had stitches before. Never broken a bone, never had anything more involved than a shot. I feel shaky all of a sudden, weak at the thought of a needle threading in and out of my lip.

She must see the fear on my face, because she puts her hand on mine and squeezes. "It's okay, sweetie. You won't feel anything after we numb it up. And it's right on the edge of your lip, so you'll barely be able to see the scar, if there even is one." I feel my eyes start to water, and she sees that too. "You want me to go get him for you? Colton? Sometimes it helps to have someone in here with you, and he's an old pro at well . . . everything."

It surprises me how much I want to say yes despite the fact that he's almost as much of a stranger to me as she is. But after seeing how uncomfortable he was out in the waiting room, I shake my head and lie for what feels like the hundredth time today. "No thanks, I'm okay."

"You sure?"

I take a deep breath, nodding on the exhale.

"All right then." She stands and peels off her gloves, folding them into themselves and then each other. "Someone will be in shortly to get you ready, and then we'll get you all patched up and on your way back out."

"Thank you."

"You bet." She smiles at me again and pats my hand. "You just promise me one thing."

I sit up on my elbows. "What's that?"

I'm expecting that she'll say that I need to be brave, or that I need to be more careful, but she doesn't. She looks at me with eyes that are kind but firm, and she says, "You promise me that as Colton's . . . friend, you'll be careful with that heart of his. It's strong, but it's fragile too." She purses her lips together for a second. "Just be good to him, okay?"

A lump rises in the back of my throat, and I bite the inside of my cheek.

"I will. I promise," I manage. Barely. My voice sounds small, scared, but she doesn't seem to notice. Or maybe she thinks it's still nerves about the stitches. She has no idea how careless I've already been, or that I know that heart of his maybe even better than he does.

She nods like we've got an agreement and pulls the curtain shut, and I lie there alone on the table, staring up at the holes in the ceiling tiles. They go blurry in an instant. I think of Colton, of how much time he spent sick. Waiting for a heart. Wondering if it would ever come, and knowing what would happen if it didn't. Knowing he would die before he really got to live.

When Trent died, I thought the worst part was that I never saw it coming. That I had no way to know we'd already had our last kiss, or that we'd said our final words, or touched each other for the very last time. I spent the first few months under the full weight of those regrets, thinking of a thousand different things I would've done differently had I known they were going to be the last.

But now I think of the way Colton changed when we walked through the hospital doors. How it must've all come rushing back at him, and I think I get it. Knowing what was coming would have been much worse.

For a moment I almost understand him not wanting any contact with Trent's family. Or with me, after I wrote him. Maybe I wouldn't want it either if I were him. Maybe I'd want to leave that whole part of my life behind too so I could get on with living the one I didn't think I was going to have.

All of a sudden it seems so selfish for me to have come looking for him. A tiny, uncomfortable question, one I'm almost scared to ask myself, tugs at the edge of my thoughts. What if I haven't been completely honest with *myself* about why I wanted to find him? I justified trying to find him with the idea that I needed to in order to move on. To find closure, say good-bye, all those things. But what if all I've really been trying to find is a way to hold on to a part of Trent? This piece I've given more meaning to than the rest, because maybe a tiny part of me feels like some essential part of him might still be there, in his heart.

It's why, an hour later, when I walk out and find Colton still in the waiting room, I steel myself against the warmth of his smile and ignore the tiny flutter it causes in my chest. It's why, when he stands without saying anything and looks at my lip and raises his hand again like he might reach out and touch it, I back away fast, put as much distance between us as possible. And it's why, when we pull up in front of his parents' shop, I don't turn off the car and I don't dare look at him. I focus only on the steering wheel in front of me.

"So we're back to where we started," he says. His words hang there between us, a flash of the morning and a beginning that shouldn't have been. All I can do now is end it.

"I'm sorry I took up your whole day with this," I say. "Thank you. For everything." I sound stiff, cold. He doesn't say anything, but I can feel his eyes trying to catch mine, and it takes everything in me not to let them. "I need to go," I say, as firmly as I can. "I've been gone for too long, and my parents are going to freak out, and I really just . . ." *Don't look at him, don't look at him, don't—*

"You wanna get something to eat?" he asks. "Before you go?"

I look at him. Wish I didn't, because his smile is all full of hope and possibility.

"I . . . no. Thank you, but I need to go."

"Oh." His smile tumbles. "Okay."

"Okay," I echo.

Neither one of us moves. Or speaks. And then we do, at the same time.

"So maybe another time?"

"It was nice to meet you."

He sits back in his seat. "I take that as a no."

"Yes. I mean, no. I can't—shouldn't."

I don't even try to explain, because I know that if I do, I'll make a bigger mess than I already have. I hate the look on his face, like I've just broken his heart. But I'm trying to be careful with it, like that nurse said, and that means ending this feeling before it has a chance to begin.

"Of all heart stories, tales of grief are most deeply etched into patients' psyches. But these losses are often buried—wounds that patients are unwilling to [fully] reveal."

—Dr. Mimi Guarneri, The Heart Speaks:
A Cardiologist Reveals the Secret
Language of Healing

CHAPTER SIX

I'M DISORIENTED WHEN I pull into my driveway, because I don't remember the drive home. I reach back in my mind for some concrete proof that I actually just drove back, but the only things I can think of are Colton's face when he bent down to the passenger window and said good-bye one last time, and the way he looked in the rearview mirror, standing in the middle of the empty street, watching my car go, one hand half raised in the air. I must've replayed an endless loop of the day all the way home—him walking into the café, his eyes and the way he looked at me. The way he sounded when he said good-bye, like he couldn't quite believe it.

The dull ache of my lip is the only thing that keeps me

from feeling like the entire day was a dream. And now I'm back. Back where I belong, and where I know my mom will be waiting, anxious and worried about where I've been. Angry when she finds out what happened. I turn off the car and sit listening to the engine settle in the otherwise still night until I'm ready to face her.

"Where have you *been*?" my mom says, rounding the corner into the entryway as soon as I walk in. "Do you know how many times I called you today?"

I don't. I've gotten out of the habit of checking my phone, or even turning it on.

I close the door softly behind me and set my purse on the entry table. "I know; I'm sorry."

Her eyes zero in on my swollen lip and the stitches, and she crosses the space between us in two steps, and she's right there, her hands on my cheeks, tilting my head back to see better, just like the nurse did. It only takes a second for her voice to go from angry to concerned. "My god, Quinn, what *happened*?"

I tear up instantly in response to the worry in her voice. "Nothing, I . . ." I take a deep breath, try to keep my voice steady, but the way she's looking at me does me in. I crumble completely, tears and all. "I ran into a car, and my face hit the steering wheel, and—"

"You were in an *accident*?" She pulls me back by my

shoulders, eyes scanning the rest of me for damage. "Why on earth didn't you call me? Was anyone else hurt?"

"No, nobody else got hurt. It was a parked car, and nobody was there, so I left a note, and—"

"Where did this happen?"

I hesitate for a moment, not wanting to have to explain why I was in Shelter Cove. But there's no way around the truth on this, not between the bus I hit and the trip to the hospital. "Shelter Cove," I say. I shrug. Teary. Pathetic.

My mom's brows crash together, creasing her forehead. "What were you doing there? Why didn't you at least leave me a note? Or answer your phone when I called? Quinn, you can't just disappear like that."

There's no way I can answer these questions honestly. Both of my parents have stuck by me since the day of Trent's accident. They've been so, so patient with me. They were even supportive of the idea of me meeting the recipients, though I knew it made them more than a little uncomfortable. I think they hoped as much as I did, or maybe even more, that all of it would help me find some sort of closure. They've given me nothing but love and time. Stood by and waited to see what I needed. Understood when I wanted space and when I needed to talk. Didn't push. But I know that behind all their patience with me there has been both the hope that I will move on and the worry that maybe I won't. Telling my mom that I was in Shelter Cove searching for the recipient of Trent's heart isn't something I can do, so I don't.

"I'm sorry," I say. "I should've told you where I was going. I just . . . had to get away for the day, and I started driving, and I ended up there, at the beach." I pause and watch her mull over this explanation, and it feels terrible, because I know what the tone of my voice implies—that it was one of "those" days when it's achingly clear that I haven't moved on, like a few weeks ago on the 365th day since Trent's death when I came home from his parents' house and didn't leave my room for three days.

"I'm so sorry," I repeat, and the tears flow again. Genuine tears, because I am genuinely sorry—for worrying her, and for using grief as an excuse this way, and for what I did today by going there. I'm sorry for all of it.

Her eyes search my face. Finally, she takes a deep breath, lets it out in a sigh. "Did you call the insurance company? Or the police?"

I shake my head, and she takes another deep breath and nods stiffly, and I know I'm pushing the limits of her sympathy.

"Why don't you go upstairs and get cleaned up, then come down for dinner, and we'll get this sorted out."

I wrap my arms around her in a grateful hug. "I'm sorry, Mom."

She hugs me back without hesitating. "I know. But you

need to be honest with me, Quinn. If you're having a hard day, and you need to get away or want to be alone, you need to talk to me. Let me know. Just be honest with me, that's all I ask."

"Okay," I say into her shoulder, and I make a silent promise to myself that I will.

After my shower and a dinner I push around my plate instead of eat, I am completely honest with her when I say that I'm drained from the day and just want to go to bed. It's too quiet up in my room, and stuffy with the day's heat. I open the window all the way and breathe in the cool air and the smell of the hills that drifts in with it. Outside, the crickets break up the silence, and the first few stars twinkle high in the dusky sky.

I cross the room to my dresser, almost afraid to look at my reflection. I avoided facing myself in the bathroom mirror, but here, alone in my room, I can't. I step in front of my dresser mirror, and my eyes go straight to my still-swollen lip, where the tiny black stitches stand out in sharp contrast against my pale skin. Proof that today happened. That I found Colton Thomas and that, despite all the rules I've come up with for myself, I met him. Spoke to him. Spent time with him. I bring my fingertips to my three stitches and wonder for a second how many it took to close Trent's heart into his chest. The thought chokes me up for too many reasons to sort out.

My eyes drift over the pictures tucked all along the edge of my mirror, silly group photos from dances, shots of us from trips with the friends we used to share. All the people I've pushed away trying to hold on to him. It didn't take long for me to realize that as much as they loved him too, their worlds didn't stop the way mine did when he died. They slowed momentarily, long enough to mourn the loss of their friend, but gradually, they picked up again. Fell back into the rhythms and routines of life. Took new pictures. Planned their futures.

A lump forms in my throat, and my eyes fall on my favorite picture of us. It was taken at one of his swim meets last spring. The sun is shining, lighting up the bright aqua patch of the pool in the background. Trent stands behind me, strong, tan arms wrapped around my shoulders, chin tucked into the crook of my neck, smiling right at the camera. I'm leaned back into his chest, laughing. I don't remember why—if it was something he said or did. And now, as hard as I try to hold on to it, I've started to forget the feeling of being wrapped up in his arms like that and the way it could make everything else disappear.

I run a finger over the glass of the frame and brush the dried sunflower hanging next to it. The very first thing he gave me, on the very first day we met. I cut the stem and put it in a vase when I got home, and after that first week of spending every afternoon together, walking back and forth between each other's houses so we could keep talking, the petals started to wilt. I hung the flower upside down then, like I'd seen my mom do, and let it dry out until it was preserved, because I knew that flower was the beginning of us. I kept it there, a reminder that I was right.

The petals are faded now, almost colorless from time and the sun, and so brittle they've started to crumble and fall away on their own. It's barely recognizable as a flower anymore. But I haven't taken it down because I can't—I'm afraid of how much I'll forget if I do.

I turn, go to my bed, and climb in; but I know I won't sleep. I don't bother to close my eyes. I lie there staring at a familiar knot in the wood of my ceiling instead, wishing I could go back to when he was here and we were together. Or that he could just be here with me, even for a moment, to remind me what it felt like, before that slips away too.

"The electromagnetic current of the heart is sixty times higher in amplitude than the field of the brain. It also emits an energy field five thousand times stronger than the brain's, one that can be measured more than ten feet from the body."

—Dr. Mimi Guarneri, The Heart Speaks:
A Cardiologist Reveals the Secret
Language of Healing

"The data [from a study entitled 'The Electricity of Touch'] showed 'when people touch or are in proximity, a transference of the electromagnetic energy produced by the heart occurs.'"

—Institute of HeartMath

CHAPTER SEVEN

I WAKE SO slowly, I can feel the layers of my dream slipping away, and I fight to keep it because I know as soon as I open my eyes, Trent will be gone, and I will be alone. Again.

Four hundred and one.

The house is so still, I know I'm alone, and then I realize

it's Saturday, and my parents are probably already out for their weekend walk to the coffee shop in town, followed by their lap around the farmer's market, before they head home for a Mom-mandated day without phones or email, working in the yard or cooking or reading together.

It's part of the campaign she started to overhaul their whole lifestyle after my dad had stumbled into the kitchen on a Sunday afternoon sounding confused, his speech garbled. She raced him to the hospital fearing the worst. After hours of tests, the doctors determined that he hadn't had a true stroke but something called a transient ischemic attack, or TIA for short. They told us it meant there had been a brief blockage of blood flow to the brain, and though there was no permanent damage, it was a major warning sign. A precursor to the real thing.

From a chair in the corner of my dad's hospital room, I watched as my mom stood next to his bed, holding his hand while the doctor listed all the risk factors: his blood pressure, cholesterol, poor eating habits, stress level, and on and on. It wasn't anything my mom hadn't already tried to tell him, but I guess it was different coming from the doctor after his attack. Changing all these things was no longer a smart recommendation but a matter of life and death.

When we got home, Dad was still shaken, but Mom had a purpose and a plan. Along with the medications the doctors prescribed, she was going to change every risk factor that could be changed. Around me, she tried to focus less on the health benefits of this "lifestyle change," but I knew what she was doing. She was fighting for my dad's life. Both of my grandpas had died before they were sixty—one from a heart attack, the other from a stroke—and she wasn't about to let history repeat itself and become a widow like her own mother. Or her daughter.

First, she hired an assistant at their accounting office and took on most of Dad's workload herself. Next, she insisted he be home each night by dinner—a healthy dinner that she cooked, rather than stay late at work and grab something on the way home like he always had. I expected him to resist and say there was too much work to be done for him to make that change, but he didn't; and that's how I knew he must be scared too. We all were. It was nine months since Trent's death, and I think even my parents were still reeling from the realization that life can be gone in an instant, without any warning at all. In a heartbeat.

Luckily, my dad had gotten a warning, loud and clear. He hadn't been at the dinner table my whole childhood, but suddenly he was there every night, obediently eating grilled fish and veggies and grains we'd never heard of. Next, Mom moved on to the weekends, which, in the last few years, he'd generally spent in his home office on the computer, answering work email and going over reports and spreadsheets, grumbling about how no one else could do any of their jobs properly. It hadn't always been like that. He used to be the one who got my sister and me up at the crack of dawn and had us out the door for a run along the rolling country roads around our house.

Now it's my mom who has him up and out early on weekend mornings. They make the long walk into town, talking and laughing together, just the two of them. Reconnecting, I guess you could say, after so many years devoted to getting a business off the ground, and getting Ryan and me to school, and practices, and meets. It's good for them both to have that connection again, and I'm glad they have that to focus on, because it takes a little bit off me. To a certain extent.

Downstairs in the kitchen my mom has left a note reminding me that Gran will be stopping by after brunch with her Red Hat ladies because she wants to spend some time with me (or because Mom asked her to babysit after my accident), and Gran needs help with a "project." Also that there's a pitcher of wheatgrass-kale morning something in the refrigerator for me. Juicing has become a part of the regimen too.

I head to the coffeemaker instead, pop in a little plastic cup, and put a mug underneath the spout. My phone buzzes from the counter, and when I pick it up, I don't recognize the number. I hesitate for a moment, think about letting it go to voicemail and then calling back later when I haven't just gotten out of bed, but I pick it up instead. "Hello?"

"Hi, may I please speak to Quinn Sullivan?" The voice is male, formal.

"This is me—she." I roll my eyes at myself. "This is Quinn."

"Oh." He clears his throat. "Hi. You, um . . . I think you hit my bus yesterday? You left a note with this number?"

"I did," I say, taking my coffee to the island. "I'm so sorry. I know I should've stayed and waited for you to get back, but I cut my lip and ended up needing stitches, and—" The doorbell rings. "I'm sorry; there's someone at the door. Can I call you right back?"

"Of course," the guy says, and I hang up without saying good-bye.

I set the phone down on the counter and head down the hallway to the front door, wishing I'd gotten dressed, because Gran's first reaction to seeing me still in my pj's when I'm supposed to be ready will be to say something about the importance of "carrying on," as she puts it, which is what she's been doing every day for the last sixteen years since my grandpa died. I pause in the entryway, smooth my hair as best as I can, and get ready for her to make a big fuss over my lip and the accident, which my mom has undoubtedly already told her about. Then I take a deep breath and open the door.

And all the air rushes right out of me.

Colton Thomas is standing on my doorstep with his phone in one hand and the other behind his back. "Hi," he says. He shifts on his feet. Gives me a tentative smile. "Soooo, like I was saying, you left me a note, and your number, and—"

Too many things race through my mind at once, too much to form a sentence; but I look over his shoulder, and there it is, the blue VW bus I smashed into, dented bumper and all.

He follows my eyes and glances over his shoulder at it. "Don't worry about that." He looks back at me. "And please don't freak out. I just . . ." He pauses and looks at his feet for a moment, then back up at me, at my lip. "I just wanted to—make sure you were okay. And to tell you not to worry about the bus. Gives me an excuse to work on it."

Finally, I find my voice, but it comes out sounding sharp. "Why didn't you tell me it was your car?"

You can't be here is all I can think.

"You were so freaked out, and I didn't wanna make you feel worse, and— I'm sorry. I should've said something."

"But how did you know where I—" *You can't be here.*

He opens his mouth to answer but hesitates. Clears his throat. "I know some people."

"At the hospital? That nurse? She told you where I *live*? I . . . you . . ."

Can't be here.

I stop myself, realizing that he's no more guilty than I was for searching *him* out. I don't know what to do with the way seeing him again makes my face go hot and my legs feel shaky. I cross my arms over my chest, suddenly too aware that I'm still in my pajamas. Look down, away from him, at the toenails I haven't bothered to polish in forever.

"I'm sorry," he says, bending a little to catch my eyes. "I'm really sorry to just show up like this. It's not—it's not something I would normally do. I just . . ." He looks at me like he did in the café, and it lets loose a flutter that starts deep in my chest and spreads out over the rest of me in an instant.

"Yesterday was . . . you were . . ." He frowns. Clears his throat and looks at the ground, my house, the sky. Finally, he looks at me. "I'm sorry, I don't know what I'm trying to say. I just . . ." He takes a deep breath and lets it out slowly. "I just wanted to see you again."

Before I can respond, he takes his hand from behind his back. Holds it out to me. And I break, into a million invisible pieces.

He looks from me to the sunflower in his hand and back again. "Um . . ."

I can't answer. I can't even breathe. My eyes burn, and the ground feels unsteady beneath me. I look at him standing there on my doorstep, a single sunflower in his hand, and all I can see is a flash of Trent. It's too much. All this is too much. I shake my head like I can make it go away.

"I . . . *no*. I can't. I'm sorry." I take a step back, start to close the door, but his voice stops me.

"Wait," he says, looking confused. "I'm sorry. That was— I didn't really think this through, I just . . . really liked meeting you yesterday, and I thought maybe . . ."

His shoulders sag, and he looks lost in a way that makes me want him to finish his sentence.

"What?" I whisper. I open the door a fraction more. "What did you think?"

He doesn't answer right away, and I don't move from the doorway.

"I don't know what I thought," he says finally. "I just wanted to know you better, that's all." The hand holding the sunflower drops to his side. "I should go." He bends and lays the flower on the doorstep, at my feet. "It was good to meet you, Quinn. I'm glad you're okay."

I don't say anything.

He nods like I did, then turns and walks slowly down the front steps, away. I look at the sunflower lying there on the doorstep. Colton walks across the driveway to his bus, and I know that if he leaves now, he won't come back and that will be the end of it. That should be the end of it. Only, in this moment, I don't want it to be.

My heart pounds louder in my ears with each step he takes, but when he reaches for his door, the only sound I hear is my own voice.

"Wait!"

The word surprises us both.

Colton freezes, and there's a second before he turns around, when I worry I've made a terrible mistake. That I've crossed a line not only with him, but with Trent too. It's not until he turns and looks at me with those soulful eyes that I realize I'm already standing on the other side of it.

"Wait," I say again, softer this time.

I don't have to say another word, which is good, because I'm still so shocked at myself I can't. Colton crosses the yard and is back up the porch steps quickly, but cautiously, like he doesn't want to frighten me off again. He stops in front of me, one step down, so we're eye to eye. Waits for me to say something more.

My mind races. *What am I doing, what am I doing, what am I doing?*

"What about . . . what about your bus?" I stammer. "How do I . . . I need to take care of it, or pay for it, or . . . something?"

He shakes his head, smiles. "No you don't. It's nothing."

"It's not nothing, it's . . ." I fumble for the right words, for any words, really. "I have to make it up to you somehow—for your bus."

What am I doing?

He turns slowly back around so he's facing me. "You don't need to make anything up to me," he says. "That's not why I came here." He shrugs and gives a little half smile. "I liked hanging out with you. So if anything, maybe just come say hi next time you're back in Shelter Cove. How 'bout that? Sometime?"

It's an invitation, but he seems to know it offers me a graceful out, if that's what I'm looking for, and the understanding of this small gesture touches me. I feel my eyes drift to his chest, and my own squeezes tight.

"Okay," I say finally. "I will—sometime."

A slow smile spreads over his face. "Sometime, then. You know where to find me, right?"

I nod, and we stand there like that with the sun beating down and the heat of the day already rising all around us. After a moment he turns to go, and this time I don't stop him. I watch as he walks to his bus and gets in. He waves, then backs down the driveway, and I stand there on the porch. A breeze rolls softly over my skin, bringing with it the scent of the jasmine and a delicate rush of something else. Hope, maybe. Or possibility. I wait until he turns onto the road and disappears to look down again at the sunflower. This time it looks different somehow—less like a painful reminder and more like a sign, maybe that Trent would understand.

This is what I tell myself as I bend to pick it up. And when I think, *Yes, I know where to find him.*

"Approximately 3,000 people in the United States are on the waiting list for a heart transplant on any given day. About 2,000 donor hearts are available each year. Patients who are eligible for a heart transplant are added to a waiting list for a donor heart. This waiting list is part of a national allocation system for donor organs. The Organ Procurement and Transplantation Network (OPTN) runs this program. OPTN has policies in place to make sure donor hearts are given out fairly. These policies are based on urgency of need, available organs, and the location of the patient who is receiving the heart (the recipient)."

—*National Heart, Lung, and Blood Institute*

CHAPTER EIGHT

COLTON'S WORDS FLOAT around me in my room as I sit in front of my computer, staring at the very first blog post I read about him. They echo, just like another set of words did, before I knew where to find him: *male, 19, California.*

Trent's family had only been given the most basic information about the recipients of his organs, and those three things were all that they knew about the recipient of his heart. That's all I knew when I wrote to him. And later, that's what I held on to when he didn't write me back. When I wanted to know where to find him, because I *needed* to know more about him.

A series of words, separated by commas, typed into a search box: *male, 19, CA*. I added *heart transplant* and got 4.7 million results in 0.88 seconds. Results I could sort by date and relevancy, narrow even further by geographic location, and still came up with endless links to follow, pieces that might or might not even have belonged to the same puzzle. I followed them all night after night, turning the pieces in the pale glow of my computer, until I found the ones that seemed to fit.

There are twelve transplant centers in California, but there was only one that had performed a heart transplant on the day Trent died. I'd found it in a blog post, written by a girl who was incredibly scared but who was trying to remain hopeful about her younger brother, who had been in the ICU there. He'd already been put on an artificial heart, but he was growing weaker every day as he waited for a new one.

I'd look at the picture on his sister's blog post, of Colton and his tired smile, flashing a thumbs-up for the camera as his parents and sister surrounded him that day, teary eyed and smiling. His sister wrote that, in this photo, they'd just heard the news that a suitable heart had been found and that, according to all the tests, it was a perfect match. This must have been about the same time when, miles away, Trent's heart was being removed from his chest as our families held each other in the waiting room, shedding tears of a wholly different kind.

The minute a heart is harvested from a donor, the clock starts, and doctors are in a race against time to get it to its recipient. The heart is sealed in a plastic bag filled with sterile solution, then surrounded by ice for transport, most often by helicopter. Trent's had been. And as it was flown to the transplant center, Colton was prepped for surgery. His family prayed, and they asked their friends to do the same, and what was life or death for them went on as a standard procedure for the doctors performing it. Just a few hours after Trent's heart had been removed from his chest, it was sewn into Colton's. Blood vessels were reconnected, and when the heart was infused with Colton's blood, it started to beat again on its own. Just as my world went completely still.

I scroll down, over words I've read so many times I could recite them from memory, to the next picture of Colton, taken just after he woke up from the surgery. He's lying on his back in the hospital bed, the ends of a stethoscope in his ears, the flat circle of it pressed to his chest by someone else's hand. Listening to his new heart beat.

It was hard for me to look at that picture the first time I saw it, so many months after Trent's death—hard not to feel the sharp pang of loss all over again. But it was impossible not to be moved by what I saw captured in that photo, and the raw emotion on Colton Thomas's face. It made me want to know him. And after months without any reply to my letter, it was through his sister's words and pictures that I started to.

I went through all of Shelby's posts and, with them, constructed parallel time lines. On the day we buried Trent, Colton had the first biopsy of his new heart and showed no signs of rejection. Nine days later, he was strong enough to walk out of the hospital and return home with his family, and I was too weak to attend the last day of my junior year without Trent. I spent the summer, and then my senior year, suspended in a haze of grief. Colton spent that time getting stronger, impressing doctors with his progress. Healing. I didn't know it at the time, but months after Trent's death, when I wrote my anonymous letter to the anonymous male, 19, from California, he was doing everything in his power to move forward and move on. And then yesterday I decided I needed to see him to do the same.

Now I don't know what comes next.

I scroll back up to the most recent post on Shelby's blog,

written weeks ago, on day 365. The anniversary of Trent's death, and of Colton's second chance at life. The beginning point of our parallel time lines. I brought them together yesterday, though that should be the end of it. There shouldn't be any "sometime." But then I think of him standing there on the porch smiling at me, with the sun shining down on us like an invitation, and regardless of what it should be, it doesn't feel like the end.

A knock on the door interrupts the thought before it can go any further. I recognize the quick, staccato raps, and I know it's Gran. I also know she'll only knock once more before she uses her key to let herself in and starts up the stairs to see why I haven't answered. She's surprisingly fast for an eighty-year-old, so I snap my laptop shut, finger-comb my hair, and get up from my desk just as I hear the second knock. I cross the room quickly, but the sight of Colton's flower on my dresser stops me for a moment. It lies right beneath the picture of me and Trent, and the now-crumbling flower *he* gave me that first day.

My eyes go straight to him, and his smile freezes me there. I tense reflexively, wait for the familiar tightness in my chest to come. But it doesn't. I glance down at the new flower again. "Was this you?" I whisper.

Though I know it's not possible, I almost expect an answer this time. But just like all the other times, the only thing I hear in the silence around me is the beating of my own heart.

An undeniable reminder of a once-unfathomable truth: that I am still here even though he's not.

"Well, look at you," Gran says, taking off her Jackie O sunglasses when I get to the top of the stairs.

"Look at *you*," I answer with a smile.

She holds out her arms and does a little spin. "Everyone always does, doll."

They have good reason to, especially today. Gran's dressed in her red and purple "full regalia," as she and her Red Hat Society ladies call it. Her feisty group of "women of a certain age" proudly wear clashing combinations as a symbol of the fact that they're old enough not to care. The glitzier the better. And Gran was born glitzy. Today she has chosen purple leggings with a matching flowing top, a red feather boa, and her signature wide-brimmed red hat with a tall plume of purple feathers that continue to float and bob in the air above her even after she stops moving.

When I get to the bottom of the stairs, she spreads out her arms and envelops me in a hug of feathers and her familiar Gran scent of Estée Lauder, Pond's cold cream, and peppermint Lifesavers. I breathe it in and hug her right back before she pulls away and takes a good, long look at me.

"How *are* you?" she asks, turning my chin from side to side. "Something is different here. . . ."

My hand goes to the three stitches in my lip, and she

waves her hand dismissively. "No, not that. That just makes your lip seem full and pouty." She angles my chin once more, turning it to one side and then the other, and I hold my breath. Gran has a way of looking at you that feels like she's actually looking *into* you, and today it makes me nervous about what she might see.

"I dunno," she says finally, dropping her hand. I exhale. "You look good today. Good enough you should've made it to brunch with me and the girls."

I smile at this. "The girls" who make up her chapter of the Red Hat Society are all seventy plus, but you really would never know it. They're a rowdy bunch. "I'm sorry," I say. "I was pretty tired after yesterday."

Gran gives a quick nod. "Well. I'm glad you're up and about. We've got work to do. Brownies. Twenty-five dozen of 'em for our booth at the fair."

"Wow."

"Wow is right. Now come help me with the groceries."

We unload the car, Gran dons her red apron as I preheat the oven, and then the two of us get down to the business of baking. It's one of my favorite ways to spend time with Gran. She directs and I follow, and we fall into a rhythm of cracking eggs, and measuring, and stirring, sometimes talking the whole time, sometimes quiet, in our own thoughts. Today we stay quiet for a little while, but I know it won't last. She waits until I pour my first batch of batter into the greased pan to start with the questions.

"So," she says, not so casually, "your mother says you had your little fender bender over at the coast yesterday? That you went driving over there without telling anyone?"

I busy myself with the spatula, scraping all the batter from the bowl, feeling bad about taking off and worrying my parents, not to mention getting into an accident.

"Were you on the prowl?" she asks with a mischievous grin.

"What?" I laugh. Her question surprises me, even though nothing about her should surprise me anymore. "On the *prowl*?"

"Isn't that what you girls call it now?" she asks as she lifts her mixing bowl with hands that tremble just a touch more than they used to. "Like a cougar?"

I hold a baking pan steady beneath it, and she pours the batter. "No. That's . . ." I laugh, wishing Ryan were here to hear that one. "That's a totally different thing, Gran. And I don't think anybody calls it that."

"Well. Whatever you want to call it. That's why *I* went to the beach when I was your age. Soon as I slipped on that bathing suit, all the boys came around." She opens the oven, slides in our two pans, and closes it. "That's how I caught your grandfather, you know." I smile at the thought of a young Gran, on the prowl for boys at the beach. "That's why he married me so fast. He saw me in that bathing suit and couldn't wait to see me out of it, if you know what I mean, and when we—"

"HOW LONG FOR THOSE TO COOK?" I interrupt.

Gran winks at me. "Forty-three minutes exactly." She starts measuring out cocoa powder for another batch, and I reach for the flour.

"I wasn't on the prowl," I say, avoiding her eyes. "I just went to get away. Do something for a change." Vague as it is, I know she'll support this reasoning.

"Well, that's good," she says. "Sometimes you've got to go off on your own. Get out. Have a day to yourself at the beach." She says it like she's proud of me, like it's a sign that I'm showing progress, or moving on, and I feel a little twinge of guilt that makes me keep talking.

"I didn't really make it to the beach—I crashed the car when I got there, so I didn't . . ."

Gran turns to me. "Well, it's the fact that you went at all, Quinn. It's a start." She carries both of our bowls to the sink and turns on the faucet. "You should go back. I tell you what—if I looked like you, I sure as hell wouldn't be spending my summer sitting in the house alone; I'd be out on the prowl." She winks again. "Or at least on the beach, in a bikini underneath that glorious sun."

She doesn't say anything else, and neither do I, and this is one of the things I love about Gran. She knows when to say just enough. And today it's just enough to get me thinking, and my thoughts drift back to Colton and his words: "You know where to find me."

I do, and I can't stop thinking about that fact.

"Maybe I will," I say after a little while. "Go back there sometime."

*"There are many things in life that will catch your eye,
but only a few will catch your heart. Pursue those."*

—*Michael Nolan*

CHAPTER NINE

BROWNIES ARE HOW I justify making the drive to Shelter Cove the next morning. I ran into his bus, and then he took me to the hospital and was concerned enough to check up on me. Sweet enough to bring me a flower. Wise enough not to push too hard. The least I can do is bring him a plate of brownies. I know from a post his sister wrote that he has a sweet tooth and that brownies were the first thing he wanted when he was allowed to start eating again, and Gran's are the best. He at least deserves that. And then I'll go to the beach.

I pile a plate high, seal it with plastic wrap, and scribble a note to my parents, who've gone out together this morning. Then I grab my beach bag and head out the door to make the same drive I did a couple of days ago, just as nervous as I was then, if not more so.

When I turn down the main street and see Colton's bus parked in almost the same spot it was the first time, my heart speeds up and I drive right by without parking in the empty spot behind it. I turn down my music so I can think better. Right now I still have a choice. If I keep driving, I haven't really done anything wrong as far as Colton and Trent go. But then. If I do that—if I keep driving—I may not get another chance to know more about him. "Sometime" will expire, and Colton will forget he said it, and maybe it'll be too late to come back.

The next light turns red. Gives me a few more moments to think. I switch on my blinker. Turn it off. Flip it again. When the arrow turns green, I hesitate long enough for the car behind me to honk, and then I make a U-turn and double back. Back to where Colton Thomas is, after 402 days. Back to where I parked the first time. When I pull in, the dent in the bumper of his VW bus is still there, and it's bigger than I remember, which makes me cringe. I glance at the plate of brownies on the passenger seat, and suddenly they seem completely ridiculous.

I don't know what I'm doing. And now that I'm here, I don't *really* know for sure where to find him. I roll down the window and look around like I might just happen to see him. The morning air is still cool, and it relaxes me the slightest bit when I take a big, deep breath. It's about the same time of day as I showed up before, and based on what Colton said, he had to mean he'd be at either the kayak shop or the coffee shop. I thought of calling him before I left, but that seemed a little much. Plus I didn't know if I was actually going to go through with it until right now, when I parked the car. In fact, I'm still not sure. The kayak shop looks closed, and even the café looks dark. I could still—

"The car's in park, right? Turned off and everything?"

The voice jolts me from my back-and-forth, and when I look up, I see Colton, fresh out of the water, hair and wet suit still dripping, surfboard tucked under his arm. "You came back." He's happy but not surprised.

"I . . . yeah."

I reach for the plate of brownies, then hold it out the window as explanation. "I brought you these—as a thank-you—or sorry, I . . ." I glance at the dent in his bumper and feel silly and embarrassed, and it makes me talk fast, all in one string of words. "You were so nice to take me to the hospital after I hit your bus, and I feel so bad you won't let me pay for it, and I know I acted strange yesterday; well, I acted strange the first day you met me too, and I—I'm sorry."

I push the plate farther out the window, like the motion can make up for the stumbling mess I feel like I am. I am rusty at this—talking to people in general. But the way he just stands there with that smile, listening to every word, makes it ten times harder.

Colton blinks once, twice, then breaks into a wide grin and reaches for the plate. "Don't be sorry. Especially not for bringing these. Brownies are my favorite."

I have to stop myself from saying *I know.*

"Thank you," he says sincerely. "You make 'em?" He leans his surfboard on the car, takes the plate from my hands, and pulls the plastic wrap back and picks out a brownie. Takes a bite. He chews slowly, like he's doing a taste test or something, and for half a second I worry that I may have messed up the recipe while we were cooking because I was thinking about him instead of focusing on the flour and cocoa powder.

Finally, he swallows. "Wow," he says, eyebrows raised. "That . . . is hands down the best brownie I've ever tasted in my whole entire life. Ever."

I feel my cheeks flush.

"I'm serious." He wipes the smile off his face to prove his point. "I've eaten my fair share."

His face is so serious, it makes me laugh. "Thank you. I . . . I'm glad you like them."

"I'm glad you came back." He smiles. "And *like* is an understatement." He polishes off the second half of his brownie. "What other secret talents do you have, and what are you doing today besides delivering the world's best thank-you apology?"

I laugh again, glance down at my lap. "I don't know. I was thinking of heading to the beach since I never made it there the other day."

"It's gonna get pretty crowded down there." Colton glances over his shoulder at the dark kayak shop. "I could show you a great little beach . . . kind of off the beaten path. Kind of a locals' spot."

"Um." I clear my throat. Entertain the idea for a moment. "No, that's okay. I don't want to take up any more of your time. I'm sure you have to . . ." I look at the shop now. "I just wanted to say thank you, and I'm sorry again about your bus." I fumble for my keys, and they fall down the crack between my seat and the center console. Of course.

"It's not a big deal," Colton says. "I don't have any other plans or anything. Let me just go change, and we can—"

"I shouldn't. I have to be home at a certain time, and I don't wanna end up somewhere far without my car and have to have you drive me back or anything like that."

He shrugs. "You can just follow me—you know, not too close because of that tendency of yours to hit the gas pretty hard. That way you'll have your car, and you can go whenever you need to." He says it so simply, like it really is no big deal, then looks at me, waiting for an answer. "It's just a day. And I need someone to share these brownies with, or I'll eat them all in one sitting. So really, you'd be doing me a favor."

He smiles, and the sunlight catches the green of his eyes, and that makes the choice for me.

"Okay. Just a day."

"Good." He grins. "Perfect." He grabs his board. "I'll just . . . I'm gonna go change then. I'll be right back." He rests a tan hand on my door, leans down, and hands me back the plate of brownies. "Here. Can you hold these?"

I take them from him, and he turns and jogs across the street to the kayak shop. Before he disappears inside, he looks back over his shoulder. "Don't leave," he calls. It makes me nervous and happy at the same time as I search for my dropped keys.

I couldn't leave now, even if I wanted to.

Each heartbeat begins with a single electrical impulse, or "spark." The distinctive sound we hear through a stethoscope, or when we place our head on a loved one's chest, is the sound of the heart valves opening and closing in perfect synchronicity with each other. It is a two-part rhythm—a delicate dance of systole and diastole, which propels the heart's electrically charged particles through its chambers roughly every second of the day, every day of our lives.

CHAPTER TEN

I PULL UP alongside the curb behind Colton, and before I can put my car in park, he's out of his and heading in my direction. I turn off the ignition and step out into the salty air, where the low sound of water crashing over rocks drifts up from below the bluff we're on.

"It's a perfect day," Colton says, looking out over the water. "Wanna check it out?"

"Sure," I say. I don't really know what we're checking out, but I'm more than happy to find out. We walk across a grassy area where a solitary old man sits on a bench reading his paper while his little dog sniffs around the ground beneath him, and when we come to the thick rope at the edge of the bluff, I get a real look at the water and rocks below.

Unlike the other day there is no fog hugging the cliffs, not a hint of a cloud in the sapphire sky that stretches huge and wide. It's the kind of day that begs you not to waste it. I feel a tiny hitch in my chest at the thought, because it makes me think of Trent. He never wasted a single second. For him it was like a clock started the moment his feet hit the ground each day. I can remember being with him and wishing that just once he'd slow down. Be still. But it wasn't in his nature to be that way, and it doesn't seem to be in Colton's either.

His fingers drum on the post in front of us, and I can feel him standing next to me, feel the nervous energy that belongs to both of us. I try to think of something, anything, to fill the quiet, but it just keeps stretching. Instead I look out over the glassy surface that surges around the enormous rocks rising out of the water. They're scattered in clusters just offshore and have always looked more like mini-islands to me than rocks. A group of territorial-looking pelicans covers the entire top of the rock closest to shore, with one taking off or landing every few seconds. My eyes travel down the craggy face of it toward the water, where it's been smoothed out by the constant surge of the waves, and I watch the water rise against the rock and then recede.

Colton clears his throat, kicks at a pebble on the ground. "So . . . can I ask you a question?"

I swallow hard. Clear my throat. "Okay," I say slowly.

He takes a sip from the water bottle in his hand and looks out over it all again, long enough to make me nervous. I think of a hundred different apologies/reasons/explanations for whatever he's about to ask me.

"You don't like questions very much, do you?" he asks, turning to me with a look that makes me fidget with my hands.

"No, questions are fine. What kind of question is that?" God, I sound as nervous as I feel.

"Never mind," Colton says, "it doesn't matter." He gives me a quick smile. "It's not a big deal, just a day. So what if we relax and enjoy it? Have one really good day?"

I flash on one of Shelby's blog posts. An Emerson quote she put up that she said reminded her of Colton and his attitude, and how he treated life after his surgery:

"Write it on your heart that every day is the best day in the year. No man has learned anything rightly, until he know that every day is Doomsday."

I remember reading it and thinking how he and I had both learned this truth, that any day could be the end. But we'd chosen to do different things with it. He put it into practice as soon as he could. Got back to the things he loved doing—the life he'd had before. I did the opposite. For so long. But standing here with him right now feels like a chance to try things his way.

"Okay," I say finally. "One really good day."

"Good. Glad that's settled." A wide, happy grin breaks over his face, and he turns abruptly and walks back toward his bus. I watch as he goes, and notice something I somehow missed before. A bright-yellow double kayak strapped to the racks on top.

A vague fear materializes in a corner of my mind as he reaches up to the strap at the front of the kayak. He undoes it quickly, moves to the back one, and lowers the kayak onto the pavement with a heavy plastic *thunk*. I glance behind me at the rocks and the swirling water down below, which doesn't seem quite so peaceful all of a sudden. When I look back at Colton, he slides the back door open and pulls out two paddles, which he sets carefully on top of the kayak. I stay where I am, in denial of all the pieces adding up right in front of me. *We're not actually, he's not thinking we're going to, I've never—*

"You ever kayak out here before?" he calls.

The man on the bench glances up, mildly interested, then goes back to his paper when he realizes the question wasn't meant for him. I cross the grass quickly, trying to think if there's a way out of this. I'm all for the beach and admiring the rocks, but kayaking through them is miles beyond my comfort zone. And it doesn't seem like something he should be doing either, with everything—it seems risky.

"Have you?" he asks with a smile. Then, without waiting for an answer, he reaches inside, pulls out a life jacket, and hands it to me.

I shake my head. "No . . . and I don't . . . I've actually never kayaked *anywhere* before, so I don't think . . . This doesn't seem like a good place to start. You know, for a beginner. All those rocks . . ." Now, in my mind, they're all jagged edges and crashing waves.

"It's actually a great place," he says. "Pretty protected. We do a lot of tours down here." He pauses with a smile. "It's where I learned."

"Really?" It comes out sounding like maybe I don't believe him, but I do. And I realize I want to know more—about him, and who he is. In his own words, not Shelby's. I can see it on his face that this is a big part of it.

"Yeah," he says. "When I was six, my mom finally let my dad take me out here with him." *Eight years before you got sick,* I fill in. *Eight years before it all started, and you went to the doctor because your mom thought you had the flu.* I feel guilty for knowing a part of his life that he doesn't realize I do, but that's not what he's thinking about right now. I try not to either. I try to be here, now, with this Colton instead of the sick one I feel like I know so well.

He shakes his head, laughs at the memory. "I'd begged my mom to let me for so long, and then when she said yes, we got here and I looked over the cliff, and I got the same exact look you did a second ago." He pauses. "I tried every excuse to get out of it, but my dad just slapped a life jacket on me, gave me the paddles to carry, and hauled the kayak down the stairs without saying anything. When we got to the bottom, he put me in the seat, and then he kneeled down in front of me and said, 'You trust your old man, right?' and I was so scared I just nodded. Then he said, 'Good. Do what I tell you, when I tell you, and the worst thing that'll happen is you'll fall in love."

I laugh nervously, try to look anywhere but at him, but it doesn't work.

Colton pauses, smiles at me with those eyes, and then looks out over the water. "With the ocean, is what he meant, that I'd take after him and want to be in it all the time, one way or another." He looks back at me. "He was right. Couldn't keep me on the shore after that day."

I know this is a version of the truth, and it's the one he's letting me know. But I also know about the years when he was sick, times that did keep him on the shore, and in and out of the doctors' offices and the hospital. Part of me wishes I could ask him about it, but the other part doesn't want to think of him that way.

"I don't really have anything like that," I say. *Anymore*, I finish in my head. I see a flash of dirt road, Trent's shoes, the two of us matching step for step, breath for breath, and guilt twists in me. "My sister and I used to run together, but she's been gone at school, so I don't really do it without her." It's the version of the truth I can let him know.

"That's too bad," Colton says. He looks like he's about to ask a question again but thinks better of it. "It's been a long time since I've been out here, but there's this cool place my dad showed me that I've been wanting to see again. It's a little tricky to get to, but worth it. You wanna try?"

I don't answer for a moment. Taking a kayak into the ocean truly scares me, but I trust him in a way that's so easy, it's almost scarier. I look away quickly, out over the edge of the bluff, down to the water swirling over the rocks, which is exactly what my stomach feels like.

"Okay. Let's try it." I don't sound very convincing.

Colton works to keep a straight face, but a smile tugs at the corners of his mouth. "You sure?"

I nod.

"You seem scared. Don't be scared. Just do what I tell you, when I tell you, and you'll be fine." He pauses and lets the smile creep slowly over his face, and though he doesn't say anything else, I can feel the rest of his dad's words swirl around in the breeze that picks up between us right then.

Colton grabs more gear out of his bus, and before I have a chance to answer, or change my mind or think things through, I've got the lifejacket on over my bathing suit, Colton is wearing a rash guard with his trunks, and we're lugging the kayak down the cement stairs to the pebbly beach. We're both a little out of breath as he pulls it to the waterline and gestures for me to sit in the front seat. I do, and he hands me a paddle. "You ready?"

"Right now? Don't I need a lesson or something first?"

Colton looks entertained. "This *is* the lesson. It's easiest to show you in the water. It's pretty small, so just get in and I'll paddle us out there. Then I'll show you. Sound good?" He smiles down at me, and I muster all the confidence I can to answer.

"Yep," I manage, but my heart pounds out steady worry in my chest as a wave breaks over the rocks in front of us, rolling them up the beach with a low *shush*. *This is actually happening.*

"Here we go!" Colton's voice says from behind me. The kayak surges forward, then rocks hard as he jumps in, knocking me off-balance for a moment. But in the next moment his weight steadies us, and I feel his paddle dig into the water on one side and then the other, and we're moving forward. I tense as a wave rolls toward us, standing up taller as it gets closer, like it's going to break before we can make it over; but Colton digs his paddle in harder, and we pass over it easily, the kayak climbing up the front of the wave and sliding down the back. Colton digs in one more time on each side and then we glide, smooth and steady over the surface of the water. Finally, I exhale.

"That wasn't as scary as you thought it was gonna be, was it?" he says from behind me.

I turn around as best I can in the stiff life jacket, surprised, and proud when I answer, "It wasn't at all."

"Little victories," he says.

I watch him a moment longer, watch him lean back in the seat and take a deep breath like he's drinking in the morning, as if doing that is a little victory in itself; and I suppose it is. It makes me feel like I do know him right then. Like in those two words is a glimpse of the kind of person he is.

"I love that," I say. "Little victories."

"They're the ones that count. Like being out here today, right now."

His words hang there between us in the bright sunlight, and I can see he means them. When his eyes sweep over the sky and the water and the rocks, and then come back to mine and rest there, green and calm, I want to tell him I know the truth. That I know why he can see things that way. I want to tell him who I am and what I was doing in the café the other day. The words all start to push their way to the surface, rising like stray air bubbles through the water.

"We're drifting," Colton says. The bubbles dissipate, and my words float away, unspoken, on the current.

He smiles and lifts the paddle from his lap, pulling me

back to the moment. "Time to learn. You ready?"

I nod, still twisted around.

"All right. You're gonna hold on to the paddle here and here, where these grips are," he says, demonstrating.

"Okay." Thankful for something else to focus on, I face forward, grab my own paddle that's been balancing on my legs, wrap my hands around the grips, and hold it straight out in front of me. "Like this?"

Colton laughs. "Perfect. Now turn back around for a sec so I can show you how to do it."

I do, and he digs his paddle into the water on one side in a strong and steady stroke that sends us gliding gently over the inky-smooth surface. Then he brings that side out and does the same with the opposite end of the paddle. "It's like you're making circles with your hands, the way you do with your feet when you pedal a bike. Try it."

He rests his paddle on his legs, and I nod and turn around to try it. The first stroke I take is too shallow, and my paddle just skips over the surface of the water. We don't budge. I feel my cheeks redden.

"Try again. Dig it in deeper."

I concentrate on using my arms to push the paddle down through the water like Colton did and am astonished when we actually sail forward a few feet.

"There you go," Colton says.

Encouraged by him and the fact that we actually moved,

I bring the first end back in deep, feeling the resistance of the water as my paddle pushes through it. I think of the circles, like pedals on a bike the way he said, and I keep going, and after a few good strokes we're cutting through the glassy surface at a decent clip. I laugh, happy and proud that I'm the one powering this little boat.

"You got it," Colton says from behind me, and I feel the forward momentum of his paddle moving through the water too. I look over my shoulder. "Just paddle," he says. "I'll sync up with you."

I nod and turn back around, face the wide expanse of blue ocean and sky in front of me, and plunge my paddle in again, and again, until I make my own steady rhythm. At first I can feel Colton's strokes working to match mine, but after a few more, we fall into a synchronized, two-part rhythm that carries us away from the shore, beyond the rock islands, out to deeper water.

A dolphin fin breaks the surface as we paddle past a patch of seaweed drifting in the sun. The only sounds are of the steady rhythm of our paddles and my breath, in and out, in and out with each paddle stroke, and I feel like I could do this forever, paddle all the way out to the horizon and keep right on going. It feels good to get lost in the natural rhythms of breath and movement without thinking of anything else. Like I used to when I ran. Until now, I didn't realize I'd almost forgotten that feeling—or that I missed it.

"I'm impressed," Colton calls from behind me. "You're stronger than you look."

"Thanks a lot," I shoot back over my shoulder with a grin. But I take it as a compliment. I do feel strong right now, and it surprises me that my body remembers how to be.

"So did you want to paddle on out to Hawaii, or do you want to see the cave?" I can hear the smile in his voice again, and then I feel the absence of his strokes. I lift my paddle from the water and rest it on my legs, noticing the burning in my arms and shoulders.

"What cave?" I ask, turning around.

"The cave we came out to see," he answers simply. I look around warily, not seeing any caves anywhere. "At the base of that rock we passed. The big one."

"Oh," I say, looking around. "I didn't see it when we went by."

"That's because it's kind of hidden."

"Like a top secret cave?" I joke.

"Sort of," Colton says with a smile. "Not part of the standard tour anyway. Too much liability. C'mon. I'll show you." He digs his paddle in deep on one side, and the kayak slowly starts to turn. "You coming?" he asks. "I can't steer this thing all by myself."

I doubt that. His shoulders are surprisingly broad, and

his arms are strong, but I turn around anyway and dig my paddle in on the same side as him, and in a few more strokes we're facing the shore again, heading back toward the rocks. It hits me right then that I've never been this far from the shore before, which is as exhilarating as it is scary.

When we were kids coming over to the coast, Ryan would swim out so far, I was always sure the lifeguards would have to go out and get her, and later on, Trent would too, racing his friends out past the buoys or the end of the pier. Fearless. But I didn't ever go out past where the waves broke. It felt too big out there, too out of control. But it doesn't today. Being out here now, I feel the best I have in a long, long time, and it makes me wish I could bottle this feeling.

Here, beneath the impossibly blue sky, I think I understand what Colton's dad meant about falling in love with the ocean. Maybe all it takes is a guide you trust.

"So those rocks all used to be part of the coastline," Colton says from behind me. I look at the rocks more carefully, and now that he's said it, I can see how their layers of color match up with the cliffs'.

"What happened?"

"Erosion," he answers. "I kinda picture it like one of those time-lapse sequences—with waves crashing against cliffs, and storms rolling over them, and water and air finding the cracks and widening them into tunnels and caves until the weak parts crumble and all that's left are these little rock islands."

The way he says it, I can see it perfectly, like it's happening right in front of us. And it is, really. Just so slowly you can't see it—the same way grief can do to a person over time, wear you down until you almost disappear.

"Anyway, the one with the cave is that one, right in front of us," Colton says.

About a hundred feet away, the largest rock of the cluster rises high up from the water. It's fairly flat on top and covered with some sort of yellow wildflowers that sway gently in the sunshine and the ocean breeze as they reach for the sky. My eyes follow a crevice, which starts out narrow at the top, down to the middle of the rock where it begins to widen into what looks like it could be an opening at the base. Water flows in and out of it every few seconds, the steady rhythm of the waves.

"It's a calm enough day; we can go in," Colton says.

I look back at the opening, which is dark and doesn't seem tall enough, weighing my bravery.

"If it's like I remember, it's one of the most awesome things I've ever seen. There's one main chamber that's open at the top, so the sun shines down into the water, and then there a couple of other smaller chambers that are all connected, and the surge pumps the water in and out of them all like—"

"Like a heart," I say. It comes out of nowhere, but from everywhere at the same time. I turn around.

Colton flinches, almost imperceptibly, but I see it and wish I could take back those three words I just said. *Stupid.* A moment ago we were out here on the ocean, just for a day, the reason for our connection left far behind on the shore. But now that reason is right here again, pulling me back in like the tide.

"Yeah," he says simply. "I guess it is kinda like a heart."

He gives a little half smile and is quiet for a long moment. I worry that he might say something about his own heart—Trent's heart.

"So what do you think?" he asks instead. "You want to go in? It's safe, I promise." His eyebrows lift in a hopeful smile.

I know it probably is safe, and I trust him, I do. But there's nothing safe about what I'm doing here with him, or the way it makes me feel, or the way he seems to trust me. Guilt tugs at my conscience, reminding me of every little wrong I've already done. But then something bigger sweeps through me, a pull toward Colton and toward this feeling I have right now.

I take a deep breath and let it out slowly, sending away all the things I don't want to think about. And then I look at

Colton, really look at him in a way I haven't yet let myself.

"I do," I say. "I want to."

He doesn't answer for a moment, just holds my eyes there in the bright sunlight. Then he smiles. "Good," he says, like it's another one of his little victories. "Because this is the part where you fall in love."

"[The heartbeat is] a link to the universal motion sur-rounding us, the tides and stars and winds, with their puzzling rhythms and unseen sources."
—Stephen Amidon and Thomas Amidon, M.D.:
The Sublime Engine: A Biography
of the Human Heart

CHAPTER ELEVEN

WE SIT A little ways off from the cavern, the kayak rising gently with each swell that passes beneath us, watching the water surge around the rock, then funnel in through the opening. I lean forward trying to see, like I have for the last ten waves, how much space there is between the surface of the water and the ceiling of the tunnel—it can't be more than a foot or two higher than our kayak.

"You okay?" Colton asks. He uses his paddle to back us up a bit. "We don't have to go in if you don't want to."

"I'm fine," I lie. But the next words are the truth. "I really want to." I count the beats it takes for the water to come rushing back out. "I just need to see it one more time, and then we can go in."

"Okay," Colton says, positioning us in front of the entrance. A few seconds later I feel another surge come from behind us and raise the kayak slightly. I watch the water funnel through the opening again. Fast.

"So remember what I said," he tells me, moving us backward while keeping us angled at the opening. "All you have to do is paddle hard, then pick up your paddle and lean way back when I tell you, okay? We're gonna catch the next wave in. And we'll make it, promise."

"Got it," I say, with far more confidence than I feel. I'm in so deep now, it's all I can do.

"Okay, here we go, right here," he says as the next swell rises behind us. "Turn around. Paddle!"

I do, and I feel the immediate power of his strokes as they join mine. Our momentum builds, and then all of a sudden we take off as the wave catches the kayak. I feel a rush of fear as it lifts us and sends us flying—right at the hole in the rock.

"Lie back!" Colton yells.

I do, pulling my paddle to my chest and screaming at the same time. It doesn't look like there's any way we'll make it through the opening, so I squeeze my eyes shut and brace myself against the sides of the kayak. Everything is loud and muffled all at once. The kayak smacks hard against the rock walls of the tunnel, knocking me around inside it. I grip my paddle like my life depends on it.

"It's okay," I hear Colton yell above the noise. "Stay down!"

At the moment, there's absolutely zero chance that I would do anything else. Even with my eyes closed I can tell it's dark. The air is heavy with moisture and salt, and it feels too thick to breathe. I squeeze my eyes shut even tighter, sure now that we're going to die because *I can't breathe, I can't breathe, I can't—*

And then a miraculous thing happens. The tunnel spits us out like the end of a waterslide, and everything goes nearly still. I lie there a moment, afraid to open my eyes, listening. I can hear my own breaths, and Colton's, and water lapping against rock, and something else . . . *dripping?*

"Ha! We made it." Colton lets out an ecstatic laugh, and then the kayak rocks and I feel a hand on my shoulder. "Hey. You okay? You can open your eyes now."

I crack one open and then the other, and the first thing I see is his face above mine. He looks down at me, and it's impossible to catch my own breath with him so close. "We made it," he says. "Look up!"

I gasp. Far, far above me I can see the sky through an opening like a skylight in the roof of the cavern. It's a window that frames it perfectly, setting off the blue in contrast with the dark walls of rock. "Oh my god," I whisper. "This is . . ." I don't even know what to call it. It's more beautiful than anything I've ever seen.

I sit up slowly, like if I move too quickly it'll disappear.

Sunlight streams in through the opening at an angle, setting the mist that hangs in the air aglow, illuminating each tiny water droplet. All around us, the water catches the sunlight and throws it against the walls of the cavern, waving and dancing. Another surge of water pushes through the opening we just came from, then disperses, rearranging the little reflections like the turn of a kaleidoscope.

I can feel Colton's eyes on me, watching me take it in. He sweeps a hand through the air, setting off tiny eddies in the mist. "When I was a kid, I used to think this was all the negative ions floating around."

"The what?" I ask, watching them swirl and dance.

"Negative ions." He laughs. "Sorry, I forget that not everyone grew up with my family and their weird random facts."

Now I really want to know. "What? What are they?"

"They're what's released into the air when water molecules collide with something solid." He gestures at the cave around us. "Like these rocks, or the beach when a wave breaks. They don't come just from the ocean, though. They can come from anywhere—a waterfall, rain . . ." He pauses and smiles a little self-consciously. "Anyway. They're good for you to breathe in. Healing, according to my dad and grandpa, at least."

He falls quiet, and I follow his eyes to the sunlit mist floating above us. We inhale deeply at the same time, and I don't know if it's the beauty of this place, or his words, or the negative ions, but I can feel something I haven't felt for a long time running through me. It's the pull of another person, of Colton, tidal in its subtlety but there beneath everything else.

"Thank you," I say suddenly. "Thank you for bringing me to this place."

A slow smile spreads over his face, and he shrugs. "I figured if all I had with you was a day, I better make it a good one."

I drop my eyes to my hands on the paddle in my lap. "You have." I look back at Colton. "It's the best day I've had in a long time, actually."

He nods, that smile still there. "Me too—you have no idea. But don't sell us short, it's not over yet."

We sit for who knows how long, breathing in the air and talking, and watching the light and the water as the cave fills and empties, until the tide starts to rise and we have no choice but to ride it out.

The surreal, euphoric feeling of the cave stays with us even after the current carries us back out into the sudden brightness of the day. It lingers in the salt air around us as we paddle in to shore and spread our towels over the pebbly beach. And it tucks itself in between us as he tells me about all the other places he plans to visit this summer, places he hasn't seen for a long time; and the earnestness in his voice makes me want to go right along with him.

I don't ask why it's been so long since he's gone to these places he seems to love so much. I already know the answer. Instead, I let myself go with him in my mind to each place he describes: a cave at the edge of an impossibly high cliff, where we can sit and hang our feet over the ledge and feel the thunder of the surf pound in our chests. A beach where the water is so clear we can paddle out and see twenty feet straight down to the colonies of purple sand dollars covering the bottom. His favorite cove, where we can watch as a waterfall plunges over a cliff onto the sand, fresh water mixing with the salt of the waves that rush up the shore. He uses that word *we* so easily, like it's a given I'm already included in his plans beyond just this day. And a part of me wants to believe it's possible.

As I lie there in the sun, its warmth sinking into the length of my body in my bikini, the truth creeps in slowly, carrying with it a wave of guilt so strong, it stings my eyes. I open them and look over at Colton lying on his back, eyes closed and face to the sky, as he describes another magical place from memory, and suddenly it doesn't feel possible anymore.

He's still wearing his rash guard, which, under any other

circumstances, might be meaningless. But I know what's beneath it. I know because I've seen it in a picture Shelby posted of Colton, bare chested, after his surgery. I almost couldn't stand to look; though at the same time it was impossible not to study the bright-red scar that ran right down the center of him. The scar from where they opened his chest to take out his sick heart and put in a strong one to save his life. The scar that I didn't realize until this moment Trent must've had too when they buried him.

I bite back tears and the terrible, awful sense that I've betrayed him in a thousand different ways by being here with Colton, and by feeling the way I did in the water: strong, and free, and . . . happy. It seems wrong, for so many reasons, that I felt happy for those moments. Happy with someone else, who is so much more than just someone else.

"So what do you think?" Colton asks, and he opens his eyes and turns his head and looks right at me, concern wiping the smile from his face. "Um. You okay?" He sits up, puts out a hand like maybe he's going to rest it on my shoulder, then takes it back, eyebrows creased with worry. "Did I— What's wrong?"

I sit up quickly, wiping the tears from beneath my bottom lashes. "I'm sorry. I'm fine. I don't know what happened, I just . . ." I can't come up with a remotely plausible explanation, so I don't try. "It's nothing."

Colton looks at me for a long moment, his eyes running

over my face, searching for what it is I'm not telling him, and I'm sure he can see it all. But then he reaches up to my cheek without a word, and this time he doesn't take his hand away. With a feather-soft stroke, he brushes away a tear, and the feel of his touch makes me wish he'd keep his hand there. I look away, out at the sparkling ocean, because I don't know what to do with the crazy swirl of emotions he's just stirred up in me.

"We should swim," Colton says. He grabs my hand, intentional in the action this time, and pulls me gently to my feet.

"What—"

"Salt water," he says, leading me to the water's edge. "Cures pretty much everything."

I sniff and wipe at my eyes with my free hand as my feet follow his. "What do you mean?"

Colton turns and looks right at me with those eyes of his. "It's a saying my dad used to always tell me and my sister— one of those things you grow up hearing all the time, so it doesn't really mean much. Until later, when it does."

"You believe that?" I ask, thinking that salt water surely didn't cure his heart.

He looks at me like it's a silly question. "Yep. It's good for the soul."

A small wave breaks over the pebbles at our feet, and the coolness of the water sends a shiver up my legs.

"Come on," he says with a smile. "It's easier if you don't think about it. Just dive in."

He's barely finished saying the words before he releases my hand, takes two running steps, and dives under the next wave. He comes up with a loud whoop, smiling and shaking the water from his hair, and seeing him in that moment, with the ocean and the sun and sky shining around him, I feel it again. The distinct pull of possibility. And I follow it. I dive in without thinking about anything else.

We swim for who knows how long, alternately ducking under waves and trying to catch them. Being in the water takes me out of my head, back into the moment when guilt can't catch me. Not even when a wave knocks me into Colton and *he* does. He catches me with one arm and then the other before either one of us really realizes, and then we're eye to eye in the water, so close I can see each little water droplet on his face. It steals my breath away, the thought I have right then.

What if we had more than a day?

"Every heart sings a song, incomplete, until another heart whispers back."

—*Plato*

CHAPTER TWELVE

BY THE TIME we climb the stairs back to where our cars are parked, the sun hangs low in the sky, spilling a golden path from the slick wet sand all the way to the horizon. I can feel the tingle of salt and sunburn on my skin as I stretch to help Colton load the kayak back onto the bus's roof racks. He cinches the straps down tight, stows the paddles in the back, and slides the door shut, but doesn't make a move to go anywhere once it's closed. Instead he leans against the side of the bus, and so do I. We linger there like that, watching the sun on the water and letting the heat from the metal sink into our backs. I wonder if he's thinking the same thing I am—that despite our agreement to keep things simple, it feels like we've shared more than just a day.

"You know," Colton says, eyes watching the sun sink lower in the sky, "the day's not technically over yet." He turns to me, that hopeful look on his face again. "Are you hungry? I know this great taco place. We could eat, and then maybe—" He stops when I shake my head.

"I can't. It's Sunday."

"You don't eat tacos on Sunday?"

I manage, barely, to match his straight face. "No. Only on Tuesdays."

We both laugh a little, but it fades quickly because we both know what's coming.

"I really do wish I could stay," I say softly. Honestly. "Sundays are family dinner, though, and my mom's a little crazy about me being there."

"I know how that goes," Colton says, trying and failing not to sound disappointed. "You can't skip out on that stuff. Family's important."

When I look at him, he gives me a smile that makes me imagine, for the briefest of moments, inviting him. But then I imagine everything that would come along with that: introducing him, and questions, and him sitting in the spot at the table where Trent used to sit, and—

I need to go now.

"Thank you so much, for today," I say, trying to sound light, but it comes out abruptly. "It really was beautiful. Everything."

Colton's smile fades the tiniest bit. "You're welcome."

I push myself away from the bus, stand up straight. "I really should go."

"Wait," Colton says suddenly. Just like I did yesterday,

just like he can't help it any more than I could.

His face is serious now. "Listen," he says. "I know earlier I said just a day, but that was . . . I wasn't being completely honest. And I know if I let you get in your car and drive away again without telling you the truth, I'll regret it all the way home."

I freeze at the words *honest* and *truth*.

He drops his eyes to the ground for a moment, then brings them back up to mine. "Anyway. I promise I won't surprise you at your door again, but if you ever decide you want another day—ever—I have lots of them, and I . . . I liked this one."

"Me too," I answer, and it's all I say, because his words, and the way he's looking at me, send little pinpricks of heat all through me. "Thank you again."

He nods, resigned, like it's the response he was prepared for. "Okay then, Quinn Sullivan. It was a pleasure spending the day with you." His tone is more polite now.

"You too." I smile. Take a few steps backward, toward my car. My heart pounds in my chest.

"Drive home safe," Colton says.

"I will. You too."

"I will."

We could go on forever like this, finding tiny, meaningless things to say to delay the inevitable, because it's not what either of us really wants. But we're each at our doors, hands on the handles, like the choice has already been made.

I stand on tiptoe so I can see him over the roof of my car, wanting one last moment. "Good night, Colton," I say.

He gives a little half smile and a quick nod. "Good night." Then he gets in his bus, closes the door, and starts it up.

I get in my car too, put the key in the ignition, but I don't turn it. I watch as Colton gives one last glance in the rearview mirror, then pulls away from the curb and raises a good-bye hand out the open window, and drives away.

I sit there in the dusky stillness of the evening until I can't see or hear his bus anymore, and then I think the words I've repeated in my mind so many times.

Come back.

Words that were a plea to Trent.

Come back.

Words that I knew asked the impossible.

"Come back."

Tonight I whisper them—to the sun setting over the ocean, to the tide carrying the moments Colton and I shared out to sea. To Colton Thomas.

"The heart is a hard flesh, not easily injured. In hardness, tension, general strength, and resistance to injury, the fibers of the heart far surpass all others, for no other instrument performs such continuous, hard work as the heart . . . enlarging when it desires to attract what is useful, clasping its contents when it is time to enjoy what has been attracted, and contracting when it desires to expel residues."

—Galen, second-century physician, "On the Usefulness of the Parts of the Body"

CHAPTER THIRTEEN

RYAN'S CAR IN the driveway is the first thing I notice when I get home. I have a moment of worry that something happened to Dad again, but then he comes around the corner of the house with the garden hose. I get out of the car, relieved but confused.

"There's my girl," my dad says, rolling up the hose as I reach the front porch. He does a double take. "You're glowing—either that or you got a pretty good sunburn."

I look down at my bright-red arms. "Time got away from me. What's . . ."

"You have a good day at the beach?"

Guilt over the half-truth in my note pings around in my chest, and I try not to make it worse by adding to it. "Yep!" My voice comes out higher than I mean for it to, but he doesn't seem to notice.

"That's great." He smiles and holds an arm out for me as I walk over. "It's good to see you getting out and enjoying yourself," he says, pulling me in for a hug. He kisses the top of my head; then his eyes fix on my lip. "You get everything worked out with the driver of the other car?"

I look at the sand that's still dusted over the tops of my feet. "Yeah, I did. He was really nice. Said there wasn't any damage to his car and that we didn't need to call insurance or anything, so it's all good."

My dad eyes me suspiciously. "You get that in writing? Because people say that stuff, and then they turn right around and file a lawsuit."

I shake my head. "He wasn't like that. He's just a local beach kid, and the van was kind of beat-up anyway. It really wasn't a big deal."

My dad raises an eyebrow without bothering to hide his smile. "Local beach kid, huh? Cute?"

"No," I say immediately. "It wasn't like that."

"Oh. He's homely then?"

I smack him on the shoulder. "No. He's not— Anyway,

what's Ryan doing home? I thought she was supposed to be on a plane to Europe."

"I saw what you just did there. We don't have to talk about the not-homely beach kid." He winks at me. "As for your sister, I don't know what's going on with her. Got here a little while ago. Hasn't said much."

"They broke up."

He nods. "I'm guessin'."

"This could be a long summer," I say, glancing at the house.

"Yes, it could."

Anyone who really knows my sister would understand. But most people don't know the real her—they know the version she *wants* them to know. She is the girl everyone looks at when she walks into the room, and the girl who walks into a room like everyone *should* look at her. At her best she is the life of the party. The kind of person who can win anyone over with her wit and natural-born moxie. But at her worst, which she likely will be if a breakup is the reason she's not going on the trip to Europe it took her two years to plan and save for, she has the ability to send the party packing. I've seen it. Lots of times.

I take a deep breath and pull my shoulders back. "Thanks for the warning."

My dad laughs. "Go say hi—she'll be happy to see you."

I reach for the door, and he gets this mischievous look on his face. "Just don't mention the nose ring—or her hair."

"*What?*"

"You'll see."

"Oh my god, Ryan, your hair—"

My sister stops chopping and holds up the hand with the knife in it. "Don't," she says. I stand there with my mouth hanging open at the fact that the hair she's always worn long and wavy down her back has been cut into an angular, asymmetrical bob, chin length on one side, shaved up the back. Definitely breakup hair. Accentuated by a tiny diamond stud in her right nostril.

She tries to keep a straight face, but a smile starts at one corner of her mouth and then she can't contain it. "I'm joking!" She flashes her full smile, the one that can get anyone to do anything for her, and sets down her knife, patting the back of her head and neck like it's still a new feeling. "Do you love it?"

"I *do*," I say, trying to match her enthusiasm, which is impossible. I'm staring, I know I'm staring, but I can't help it. "It's just so . . . different," I say, "but it looks really good on you."

I'm being honest—it does. The hair shows off the graceful curve of her neck, and the tiny stud highlights her cute little nose just perfectly. She looks beautiful and tough at the same time, which I'm guessing is the goal.

"Thanks," she says, coming over and pulling me into a tight hug with her thin arms. She smells like the fresh basil she was chopping, and the same Body Shop perfume oil she's used and I've swiped from her for as long as I can remember, and it makes me glad. At least she smells the same. "It's such a stereotypical thing to do, I know, but I *love* it. It was time for a change."

"So you and Ethan . . . I'm sorry—"

"Don't be," she says, releasing me from the warm grip of her hug. "I was done being his manic pixie dream girl, and I sure as hell wasn't gonna follow him around Europe making sure he was content with life."

"You weren't gonna be his what?" I ask. It's hard to picture her following anyone or being anything other than what she wants to be.

"His manic pixie dream girl," she says, straightening her small shoulders. "It's this totally sexist feminine trope we studied in my Women's Studies class this semester, and it completely opened my eyes to the fact that I've been exactly that to Ethan this whole time. Actually, I think I might've been that to all my boyfriends." She goes back to the cutting board on the island and starts chopping again. With a vengeance.

"Been *what*?" I'm not entirely sure what a trope is, but she sounds pissed about it.

She sighs, like I'm testing her patience the tiniest bit. Or like there's a lot I need to learn. "Just an idea of a girl—you know, the quirky, cute girl who swoops in and shows the sensitive, slightly nerdy guy how to live and enjoy life? That girl."

I can tell by the way she says it that she thinks it's a bad thing, so I avoid pointing out to her the irony that right now, madly chopping basil, with her new haircut and the tiny stud in her nostril, and combat boots and little cutoffs, she looks a little manic and a little pixie.

"I was just this *idea* to him," she continues, waving the knife as she says it, "and now I'm not." She balances the cutting board on the rim of a large bowl and uses the edge of the knife to scrape the pulverized basil into the tomato salad. "It's better this way."

I reach over to the bowl and risk losing a finger to pick out a grape tomato. "But what about your trip? Did you lose all your waitressing money?"

"I'm probably out a plane ticket, which sucks, but the rest was just gonna be hostels and cheap places we found once we got there. I have plenty left." She pauses. "I'll find somewhere else to go on my own. Maybe Morocco. I'll swim in the turquoise water and ride buses from town to town with locals, and buy cheap jewelry in outdoor marketplaces, and get drunk on weird foreign drinks, and kiss beautiful boys who speak broken English and want to please *me*." She twists the pepper grinder over the bowl. "Either that or I'm applying for a study abroad year at that art school I wanted to go to in Italy."

"How much to cart an old lady along with ya? Either place?" Gran asks from the kitchen doorway. I wonder, mainly for Ryan's sake, how long she's been standing there.

"Graaaann!!!" my sister squeals, and rushes over to our grandma, squeezing her in the same tight hug she gave me a few minutes earlier.

Watching them, I can see what everyone has always said. They are two peas in a pod, only they're separated by sixty years. It's a quality I can't put my finger on, a confidence in the way they carry themselves, just naturally. But it must've skipped around the genes in the family, because my mom doesn't have it, and neither do I.

Gran steps back from the hug and surveys Ryan's latest incarnation at arm's length.

"Give it to me straight, Gran. What do you think?" Ryan says. She sticks out her small chest, comfortable, and even a little proud to be judged.

Gran looks her up and down one more time. "Sassy. I like it. Except for that little thing in your nose. Looks like you need a hankie."

Had any other person in the world said that to my sister, they would've known her wrath. But since it's Gran, Ryan bursts out in a laugh that fills the kitchen and makes it impossible not to join in.

Gran turns and walks around the island to me then, laying a slight but gardening-rough hand on my cheek. "And what about you, my dear? I see you have a new look too."

I look down at my sundress and sandals, and I'm a little proud to tell her. "I went to the beach."

"On the prowl?" she asks.

I shake my head.

"Well it looks good on ya," she says, her hand motioning in a circle in front of me and sweeping down to my sandy toes. "This. The sunshine, and sand, and sea."

"Thank you," I say, a little nervous. Unlike Ryan, I'm *not* comfortable being looked at so closely. Probably because it feels like that's what everyone has done with me since Trent died. And because right now it feels like Gran can see straight through my sunburn. "I went kayaking," I add. "Took a lesson."

What am I saying?

"*Really?*" Ryan raises an eyebrow as she hands me an ear of corn.

I set to work peeling the husk and wishing I could take back my involuntary confession.

"That's *won*derful, sweetheart," Gran says, using a much more delicate tone with me than she does with my sister. Like I *am* more delicate than my sister. She gives my cheek a gentle pat. "If you enjoyed yourself, you should take it up. Get out there on that ocean and live in the sunshine, and swim in the sea, and *drink* that wild air. That's what I always say."

"That's Emerson, Gran. It was on the birthday card I sent you last month," Ryan says, drizzling olive oil over the caprese salad. Only she could get away with calling my grandma out.

"Great minds then, Emerson and me," Gran says. She opens the fridge and takes out a bottle of white wine, turning back to me. "Anyway, doll, I'm happy to see you doing something like that. I think it calls for a little celebration, in fact." She puts the bottle under the opener and uncorks it with a low pop, right on cue. Then she pulls a glass from the cabinet and fills it far beyond what most people would consider acceptable.

Ryan laughs.

"What? No sense getting up to refill it in five minutes," she says with a wink. "I'm old. I've earned the right to sit and enjoy a glass of wine with my two beautiful granddaughters."

It's all the invitation Ryan needs. She takes down two more glasses and pours her own glass, finishing off the bottle. I give her a look, which makes Gran laugh.

"What?" Ryan says. "It's what I'd be doing in Europe right now anyway."

Gran raises her glass and clinks it with Ryan's. I grab a

bottle of mineral water from the fridge and fill my own glass.

"To new beginnings," my sister says, and she raises her glass my way, giving me the distinct impression she's not just talking about herself.

"To new beginnings," Gran repeats.

A little rush of guilt rolls through me, and I can't quite say the words; but I do manage to raise my glass, and between the soft crystal clink it makes against theirs and the evening light slanting in through the kitchen window, there is something comforting and hopeful about those words. I take a small sip before I set down the glass.

Gran smacks me on the butt. "Now go get washed up for dinner. I don't want to get in trouble with your mom. She already blames me for the way this one turned out."

Ryan just smiles and takes another sip of her wine like it's an everyday thing for her.

"Fine," I say, trying to sound exasperated, but they make me happy, these two together. "Where is Mom anyway?"

"She dropped me off and then went to that hipster organic market to pay three times the amount she would at the grocery store for grass-fed, massaged, blessed, heart-healthy meat to feed us all."

Ryan and I catch each other's eye—Gran just said *hipster*.

"Trendy hipster markets," Ryan says with a smirk as she puts the salad in the fridge.

"What a racket," Gran agrees.

I finish husking the last ear of corn, put it on a tray, and look around for another dinner task that'll stretch out my time here in the kitchen with the two of them, because I realize right now in this moment how much I love my gran, and how much I've missed my sister. Having Ryan back is like having a whole different level of energy in the house.

"Go on." Gran shoos me. "I need to talk to your sister about her liberation from the angry pixie trope." She gives me another smack on the butt, and I turn to head upstairs, knowing she wants a few moments alone with Ryan.

For all the bravado each of them has, I know exactly how it's going to go. Gran will want to make sure Ryan's really all right, and she'll make her give it to her straight. Ryan will let herself be upset with Gran if she needs to be, and then they'll build their strong front back up together. It's been their thing since Gramps died when I was seven and Ryan was nine.

Neither one of us had ever seen Gran so completely distraught before, let alone rendered paralyzed and silent. She was—and still is—always moving, always busy, always doing *something*. But when my grandpa died, she just stopped. I didn't understand it then, but now I've known the feeling for too long.

When it happened to Gran, I skirted the edges of whatever room she was in while Mom took care of necessary details day in and day out. I didn't know what else to do. But after a few weeks, Ryan marched right up to Gran one day as she sat in the chair she seemingly hadn't moved from since the service. Ryan put her hands on her hips and gave Gran an order. "Get up."

Somehow those words snapped Gran out of her grief-induced paralysis, and ever since, the two of them have had this understanding and this toughness with each other that I wish they'd try with me too. Instead, when Trent died, everybody tiptoed around, and doted on me, and acted like I was made of glass. They didn't need to worry about breaking me, though. I was already shattered all over the floor into tiny slivers—the kind that escape the cleanup and come out of nowhere, invisible little things that surprise you when you least expect them.

I step gingerly up the first few stairs, hoping to catch some of the words that pass between Ryan and Gran, but their voices are hushed now, so I give up and head to the bathroom to shower. With the door closed and the shower on, I pull my sundress over my head so I'm in my bikini, and I look at myself in the mirror that's already fogged up around the edge. I look for what my grandma was talking about, and I almost think I can see it—something different, courtesy of the fresh air, and the ocean, and . . . and maybe Colton Thomas too.

My dark hair falls wavy and wild over my shoulders and

chest, which are both a deep red that I know will fade to tan tomorrow. I lean in closer and can see, just barely, that there's a new sprinkling of tiny freckles across the tops of my cheeks and nose. I smile at my reflection before it fades behind swirls of steam. I had a good day. For the first time in a very long time, I really did, which is why I almost don't want to wash it away tonight. I like the feel of the salt and the sand on my skin, like a reminder that there is a whole world that's alive and continuing on out there.

And that today I was a part of it again.

"The hand cannot execute anything higher than the heart can imagine."

—Ralph Waldo Emerson

CHAPTER FOURTEEN

"SO WHAT ABOUT that kayak lesson you took today?" Ryan says brightly as she passes me a platter piled high with foil-wrapped corn. I feel Mom's ears prick up, and I shoot Ryan a look.

"What?" she asks innocently. But there's a tiny flicker behind her eyes that asks me to go along with it. "I think it's awesome that you did that."

And you don't want to talk about Ethan or your trip or why you're here right now, I think.

"What was that now?" Mom asks like she didn't hear Ryan quite right. "You took a *kayak* lesson today?" She looks at me, confused. And rightly so. This *is* out of left field for me. "Was this with you?" she asks, looking at Gran. "A Red Hat thing?" Gran shakes her head, and Mom looks back at me, even more confused. "Who did you go with?"

I pass her the corn platter and take the plate of hipster-market steak from Ryan, trying to sound casual about it. "It was just me, by myself. Gran and I talked yesterday about doing something like that, and so today I just—I just did it. On a whim," I add, trying to say it like Ryan would—with enough resolve and confidence that no one questions it, never mind the fact that kayaking isn't something I've ever shown any interest in. Ever. Mom used to catch all those details, but since Dad's stroke scare, she's been a little less astute with that kind of thing.

Either it works or it's a story they're all more than willing to go with anyway, because then comes a series of questions, like I've just returned from circumnavigating the globe rather than from a kayak lesson on the coast. Everybody talks over one another while passing food and dishing up their plates. All except Gran, who sits with a wry little smile watching the interrogation.

Dad: "Did you have a good time?"

Mom: "You didn't get your stitches wet, did you?"

Ryan: "Was your instructor a guy?"

Dad: "Where'd you go?"

Mom: "You could get an infection that way."

Ryan: "Was he cute? Single?"

"Wow," I say, once they've all got their questions out. "It was just a kayak lesson." It comes out sounding irritated, and I know it's because I'm mad at myself for stretching the truth and omitting one extremely important detail of this story. Why did I have to say *anything*?

Mom smooths her napkin in her lap. "I'm sorry, honey. I think we're just happy to hear that you enjoyed yourself today. It's exciting," she says with a smile and a little raise of her shoulders. I know she's right, and I feel bad that me getting dressed and leaving the house is now cause for celebration.

"It's not a big deal," I say, more to my plate than to her, like I don't know they watch me every day to see if this will be the one when I finally start to move on.

Gran cuts in. "What your mother's trying to say, all BS aside, is, we're happy to see you beginning to—"

"Carry on?" I finish with her two favorite words.

"Exactly," she says, setting down her fork. "So *my* question for you, Quinn, now that the peanut gallery is finished, is, have you made plans to go again? I think you should, if you know what's good for you. I'm old enough to know. Strike while the iron is hot."

"Or the kayak instructor," Ryan adds under her breath.

"Ryan," Mom warns.

"I don't know." I shrug. "I haven't made any definite plans." I pause, and for a moment let myself imagine pulling up in front of Colton's shop, walking in, and telling him I'd like another day. With him. "Maybe," I add, and saying it out loud makes me nervous.

"Oh, don't give me that 'maybe' crap," Gran says. She takes a dainty, pinkie-raised sip from her wine glass and nods as she swallows it. "Do it tomorrow, or you never will."

Mom gives Dad a look I know means she's had it with her own mother, but I like it. It's like Gran thinks I can finally handle a little tough love.

"She's right," Ryan says, "Why would you not?"

Why would you not?

I hear Colton saying those same words in the café, and I can think of so many reasons why I definitely *should* not. But they're getting harder to hold on to, especially with my family's reactions.

"What do you think?" my mom asks. "Why don't you give it another try? We're all busy tomorrow, and it'd be better than sitting in the empty house all by yourself, spending hours on the computer searching for . . ."

Searching for that heart recipient.

Everyone goes quiet for a moment, and I wonder what they would think if they actually knew. If they knew what it was they were encouraging me to do.

"It'll be my treat," Dad says. He raises his beer like we're doing a toast.

I look at my family for a moment, at all the hope on their faces. Like this could be the thing that will finally snap me out of it. And I can't say no.

"Okay, okay, I'll go again," I say, sounding more certain about it than I am. I'm not sure if I really intend to go kayaking again, or to see Colton again to do that, but I can drive over to Shelter Cove and spend the day at the beach and come back letting them think I've taken another lesson if it'll make them happy.

"Tomorrow?" Gran asks. She arches a single brow at me, implying the answer she wants.

"Tomorrow."

"It's settled then," she says with an authority no one challenges.

And just like that, we all go back to dinner as evening deepens around us out on the deck. Crickets chirp in the background, and all of Mom's candles in their Mason jars flicker and dance as talk turns to Ryan and what her summer plans are now that she's home. They talk about trying to get her plane tickets refunded, the possibility of her spending a year abroad at the Italian art school she's so excited about, the safety of traveling alone in Morocco. Dad's next checkup. Mom's latest health fact. Gran's next Red Hat Society meeting.

I don't say much, and they don't seem to notice, maybe because I've been quiet for so long, since Trent. Tonight's different though. Here, with my family and their good intentions all around, I'm not wishing I could go back. I'm not replaying the past. Tonight I let myself drift away, back to the ocean and a kayak, and the possibility of another day with Colton. I know it's dangerous, what I'm doing, but I think about how it felt being with him today, and the truth is, I want to feel it again.

After the dishes have been cleared and washed, the food put away, and Gran taken home, I tell my parents I'm tired from my big adventure and leave them sitting on the back deck by the pool, a candle flickering softly next to the two glasses of wine on the table between them, night falling soft and blue all around. I pause once I'm inside and look at their silhouettes through the window. They're nodding and talking, and my dad reaches across the table to rest his hand on Mom's arm. She leans toward him and laughs, and seeing them together like that brings on one of those moments that hit me out of nowhere.

I can't remember the last time Trent and I sat like that. I can't remember the last time he was at our house for Sunday dinner. He came almost every Sunday, so it would've been less than a week before he died. But I can't remember it. All the nights he spent at our table with us have blurred together, become fuzzy around the edges. I can remember the easy way he chatted with my parents, complimenting my mom on her cooking or offering to help my dad with whatever big yard project he had going on. The way he always joked with Gran about her Red Hat ladies and their antics and teased Ryan like she was his own sister. The way we'd stay out on the deck long after everyone else. His arm resting on the back of my chair, my head on his chest, we sat watching stars appear in the sky.

I can remember all those things. But I can't remember the last time he was at our house for Sunday dinner.

I'd give anything right now to go back, even just for a few moments, so I could pay more attention. Inscribe every detail of him, and of us together, onto my heart, where I could keep it safe always. Where even time couldn't erase it.

My body feels heavy as I climb the stairs to my room, and all I want is to tumble into bed and fall into the kind of sleep where I can dream about Trent; but I hesitate when I get to the top of the stairway. Ryan's already in her room, and I can hear the muffled beat of music escaping along with the slice of light from under her door. All of a sudden my room looks too dark in contrast. Too quiet. I want to be in the light and energy and music of my sister's room, such a welcome difference from the stillness of mine for the last nine months while she was away at school.

I knock tentatively because she used to always make me. I'm not sure if the same rules apply. So much of her is the same, but so much is different too. Ryan has a new air about her, like she's a level removed from this life here, which I guess is true after being away.

"Come in," she calls from behind the door.

I open it just wide enough to poke my head through.

"Hey," I say, realizing I don't really have a specific reason to be here.

"Hey," she echoes, giving me a funny look. "Come in. What's up?"

I open the door wider but stay in the doorway, still feeling a little unsure. "I don't know; I just . . ." I smile. Try to think of something else to say. "I'm glad you're home."

"Me too," she says, turning down the music. She looks me over carefully until her eyes rest on the stitches in my lip. Her brows come together. "How are you doing? I mean really. Like, not the Mom answer, the real answer."

She pats the bed next to her, and I realize that is exactly what I was hoping for when I knocked on her door. I step in and pull the door closed until I hear the tiny click, shutting me into the cocoon of my sister's room.

I want to tell her about today, and about Colton, and the cave, and the feeling of being out on the ocean. The feeling of being with him. But I know if I do, she'll ask questions—too many, and I don't want to have to lie to her to answer them.

I don't say anything.

She scoots from the middle of her full bed to one side and pushes aside a messy stack of magazines to clear a spot for me. "Sit. Talk."

I sit. "I'm all right," I say. I don't sound convincing even to myself.

"Really?" she asks flatly. "You still have pictures of you and Trent up in your room."

There it is. That direct approach I wished earlier that she'd use with me. I take it back. Get up to leave. "What were you doing in my room?" I'm surprised at how uncomfortable this makes me all of a sudden.

"Wait," she says, a firm hand on my shoulder. "Don't get mad—I just poked my head in when I got here, and I saw them still there, is all."

I sit back down on the edge of the bed with my back to her. The bed shifts with her weight, and her arms come around my shoulders. "It's like a time capsule in there. A really sad one."

I don't answer.

"Maybe . . . ," she says gently, "maybe it's time to . . ."

Tears spring to my eyes, hot and angry, and I turn to face her. "To what? Take them down and act like he never existed?"

"No," she says, more firm now than gentle. She reaches out to put a hand on mine, but I pull away. "That's not what I meant." She sighs. "Just . . . doesn't it make you sad to look at them all the time?"

I wipe my eyes, hating that even after this long, tears spring up so readily. "It's not the pictures that make me sad." It's that without them, all those little details about Trent will start to fade.

"I know that. Believe it or not, Quinn, we all loved him, and we all miss him, still. I know it's on a whole different level for you, but I think . . ." She pauses, and I can tell she's trying to choose her words carefully. "I think you're making it hard for yourself to move on. At all. Mom told me about all the letters, and meeting the recipients, and you looking for the heart guy. She's worried that you've been stuck on that—finding him—and it just seems . . . like maybe you need to let go a little."

I bite my cheek hard, and I can feel my shoulders stiffen.

She moves in front of me now, so I have to look at her. "Finding the guy who got Trent's heart isn't gonna bring him back. Neither is acting like you died too."

Anger flares up in me, hot and stinging. "You think I don't *know* that?"

She doesn't answer, just presses her lips together like she doesn't know what to say to me. Like I'm different now too.

"I know that," I say softer, unsure of myself all of a sudden because I see Colton standing there on the front steps with the sunflower in his hand. I think of the way being with him felt so easy and familiar, and all of a sudden it makes me question my own feelings. Makes me wonder why I'm so drawn to him.

I look down at my hands twisting in my lap. "I'm not trying to bring him back. I was just trying to . . ." I stare at the magazines spread all over her bed and think about how to explain what I mean, what I was actually trying to do by reaching out to the people Trent helped, though I'm not sure I know anymore. I thought it was for closure. But this, with Colton, is different.

I push the thought away and pick up a picture of a white-sand beach.

"What is all this?" I motion at the mess spread over her bed by way of changing the subject. There are pages torn out of magazines: pictures of beaches, exotic-looking cities, a Japanese garden, an art museum, a lake like a mirror that reflects the mountains and sky all around it. There are words cut out too, in all different sizes and fonts: *create*, *be bold*, *live free*. . . .

"It's for a vision board I'm making," she says, maybe just as relieved as I am to change the subject.

"What's a vision board?" I ask, wiping the wetness away from my eyes. "Does it have something to do with the manic pixie thing?"

Ryan laughs. "No, not really." She thinks about it. "Well, sort of. It's an inspirational tool. A way to visualize what you want so it's easier to focus on." She sifts through the stack she's cut out already. "You choose pictures or words of things you want to do, or be, or have, or things that inspire you, and you put them all up where you can see them every day, to remind you and keep you moving toward them."

She's quiet a moment, and I'm sure it's because she's

thinking of the photos I have up in my room, the pictures of Trent and me together that I look at every day. Pictures of things I can't have anymore because they exist only in the past.

"Did you learn that in your Women's Studies class too?" I say, not wanting to veer back into our previous conversation.

She grins. "No. From my New Agey roommate. She's all into that stuff. Here," she says, handing me a magazine with a sun-soaked cover. "You should make one. Start with this. Travel is easiest. Find a beautiful place you'd wanna go and cut it out."

When she says it, the first thing I think of is the inside of the cave today, with the reflection of the water dancing all around. And Colton sitting across from me. I want to go back there. I doubt I can find a picture that comes close to being that beautiful, but I take the magazine anyway, and Ryan sits back with hers, and we skim our magazines without saying anything else.

She grabs a pint of cookie dough ice cream from her nightstand, takes a bite, and passes it to me. "Eat. You're too skinny these days, and Mom's gluten-free, sugar-free tart thing couldn't pass for dessert anywhere."

I laugh. "Oh my god, you have no idea the things we've eaten since you've been gone," I say, digging into the middle, where all the cookie dough is.

"Well, eat up." Ryan smiles. She reaches for another magazine. "Then pass it back."

I can't remember the last time the two of us sat together like this, but it feels just right being in her room, sharing a spoon and a carton of ice cream and flipping through magazines. It feels normal.

I sneak a glance at Ryan, who is busy cutting out pictures and words with abandon, sure of herself like always. Focused on seeing her future instead of her past. Right then I wish I could snap a picture of *her* and put it up as inspiration to do the same thing.

I page through the first magazine aimlessly, unsure of where to start. Truthfully, I haven't thought about the future a whole lot in the last 402 days. And the things I used to want seem so trivial and faraway now anyway. Had I been sitting here in Ryan's room *before*, I probably would've torn out pictures of what I wanted my senior prom dress to look like, of the college Trent and I would go to together, a ring I'd imagine him giving me somewhere down the road, or the house that we would have. I would've made a collage of the life we'd have together. That's what you do when you think you've found your one true love.

I still don't know what you do when you've lost him. I stopped running, didn't go to senior prom. I pushed all our friends away until they stopped calling. Mom and Dad made me go to graduation, but I walked out when they started the slide-show tribute to him. I missed college application deadlines and didn't care. I've spent the better part of the last thirteen months alone and stalled out, an eighteen-year-old widow who has yet to make plans or look forward no matter how much anyone tries to get me to.

I page through more magazines, one after another, past words that don't speak to me and pictures that don't stand out as anything I want, or even think is a possibility. Until I get to one that stops me. I run my eyes over the picture, take in all the details: clear water and sunset-gold light, velvety-looking sand, and a lonely bottle washed up on the shore. It's what the bottle contains that gets me. Inside its clear glass sits a deep-red, blown-glass heart. The sun shines through it at just the right angle so that it throws a small red shadow on the sand in front of it. I've never seen anything like it. The heart is beautiful, and fragile, and safe inside its bottle, like the old notes that supposedly traveled over distance and time, through storms and lulls, to finally find a shore. And then to be found.

"The average heart beats eighty times per minute, which means that, in any given day, your heart will beat approximately one hundred thousand times. In a year, it will have beaten forty-two million times, and in a lifetime it will beat nearly three billion times. All the while, it is taking in blood and expelling it to the lungs and throughout the body. . . . It does not rest. It does not tire. It is persistent in its drive and purpose."

—*Dr. Kathy Magliato,* Heart Matters:
A Memoir of a Female Heart Surgeon

CHAPTER FIFTEEN

"GET UP."

I don't need to open my eyes to know Ryan's standing next to the bed. She pulls my covers off, and I scramble to get them back. "Are you crazy? What time is it?"

"Six," she says. "It's gonna get hot early, so get up. We're going for a run."

I squint at her, already in her running gear, in the pale morning light. "Seriously?"

"Seriously."

"I don't have any running shoes," I say, reaching for my covers.

"Really?" Ryan crosses my room, opens the closet door, and climbs into the back, where every Saucony I've ever owned is piled. Shoes start flying, one after another, each landing on the carpet with a thump.

"I'm sure two of these will work," she says. Then she heads to my dresser and pulls out shorts, a tank top, and a sports bra. Tosses them on the bed. Next, my sister crosses the room, pulls up my blinds, and lifts the window wide open, letting the cool morning air in. She pauses a moment to breathe it in, then grins at me. "C'mon. Get yourself up—it'll feel good. Dad's waiting." Then she leaves the room—her favorite way to end a discussion.

Dad's waiting? It's been even longer since he's gone running than me. Longer than 403 days. The number comes to mind automatically, but not with its usual weight. Today feels different because yesterday was different.

I stretch my arms above my head, wincing a little at the unexpected soreness in my shoulders. And then it all comes back to me: paddling with Colton, the sunshine, the water, his hand waving out the window as he drove away. The empty feeling that good-bye left me with. And then later, the dinner discussion with my family about going back today.

My phone buzzes on my nightstand, and I jump at the sound. I reach for it, hoping it's him and telling myself at the same time not to hope, that I'm being ridiculous. But when I look down at the screen, it's a text from a number I recognize now. I freeze. Stare at until it buzzes again in my hand, and then I swipe it open.

> So I was thinking. Yesterday was a really good day, but I bet today could be even better. What do you think?

I smile, and my first thought is that it already is. Another text buzzes through:

> Working at the shop this morning, but maybe later we could see?

I read the words over again, trying to think of how to answer.

"*Quinn.*" Ryan pokes her head through my doorway, and I jump again, not sure what to do with the phone in my hand. "What are you doing? Let's go."

I put my phone back on the nightstand. "Nothing. I was just turning off my alarm."

"Well, come on; get up. We're waiting on you." I know she's not going to leave again until I actually get out of bed, so I do. Answering Colton's texts will have to wait, because my sister does not.

Mom's in the kitchen, dressed for work, when I get downstairs. "Good *morning*," she says brightly, setting down her green juice and reaching out her arms for me.

"Morning," I answer.

I shuffle over and give her a quick hug. She kisses the top of my head. "It's so nice to see you up. And dressed. Your dad's going to be so happy. This'll be his first run in *years*." I can see how hard she's trying to contain how pleased this makes her. Never the runner, but always the cheerleader, she's beaming, back in her old role.

"They're waiting outside," she says. "I'm heading in to work early and won't be back until around five. Have a good day, and have fun running and kayaking!" She gives me another kiss on the head and squeezes my arm, and I can feel the hope in it.

"Quinn!" Ryan yells from outside. "You coming?"

I don't answer, just head out to the front porch, where she and Dad are waiting. She's got one leg slung up on the railing, and she stretches over it, grabbing her toes easily.

Dad laughs when he sees me. "Well, good morning, Sunshine. Looks like your sister's powers of persuasion worked on you too, huh?" He gives my ponytail a tug.

"Something like that." I shake out my legs and stretch a little.

My dad looks from me to Ryan, and then wraps an arm around each of us, pulling us out of our stretches and into him for a hug like he used to when we were younger, so close our cheeks almost smoosh together. "This is a treat for your old man, you know that? Like the old days. Except now you two are gonna have to wait up for *me*. I've been walking with your mom, but I don't even wanna think about how long it's been since I've run."

I know exactly how long it's been since I've run, but *I* don't want to think about that. Instead I go back further, to before I ever knew Trent, to when Ryan and I started running with our dad. She was fifteen and I was thirteen, and those runs with him were special. They were for summer and weekend days, when he still had the time. He'd get us up and out the door early, never telling us where or how far we were running, but he always made sure there was a cool destination involved. Something to show us, like the top of a ridge where you could see all the way to the ocean, a tunnel made of oaks and hanging Spanish moss, vineyards that stretched and rolled for miles with bitter little grapes we'd pick as we went, a trail off the beaten path where we'd see deer, and wild turkeys, and rabbits. Ryan and I always made a big deal of groaning about getting up, but we both loved those runs with him and the things he showed us.

"I don't know, Quinn's a little out of practice." Ryan looks at me, a hint of challenge behind her smile. "I think we both might finally be able to kick her butt."

I feel an old fire start to flicker. A competitive one. Ryan and I both ran cross-country and track, but I made the varsity team as a freshman, and I was always a little faster. It drove her crazy, and it was one of the things I loved best about running. That it was mine. My place to shine when she did everywhere else.

Dad shakes his head. "We don't need to race or anything. We'll just go slow and get the feel of it again." He catches my eye. "With something like this, you've gotta ease back in." The way he looks at me, I know he doesn't just mean physically.

More than once after Trent died, he asked me if I wanted to go for a run together even though he wasn't really running anymore either. It had always been our special time before, and I think he was looking for a way to find that again—to check in with me, because we hadn't ever talked about that morning after the fact. He'd been the one the paramedics handed me over to and the one who'd driven me to the hospital, chasing the ambulance with its swirling lights. But after that day I was so far lost I couldn't talk to him any more than I could run past that stretch of road.

"Okay, we go easy," Ryan says, "but I choose the route."

"Deal," Dad answers.

"Good. I have an idea of somewhere I wanna go." She looks at me with a grin. "It's a little tough but nothing you can't handle."

I take a deep breath. Hope I can still rise to her challenge.

She bounds down the stairs, and Dad and I follow. I'm not sure she's right about me being able to handle it, but I hope so. I take another deep breath as my running shoes crunch over our dusty driveway. Ryan starts jogging right away, and so does my dad, and then I have no choice. We head down our driveway at a slow warm-up pace that feels clunky, like my body doesn't remember how to do this anymore.

Ryan pauses, and for a second I freeze up at the thought of running by that place on the road, but she knows better than that and turns in the opposite direction. We fall into a single-file line on the narrow shoulder, with Ryan leading, Dad in the middle, and me bringing up the rear. I focus on putting one foot in front of the other, not just because I need to if I want to keep up, but because Trent is the first thing I think of once we get going. I was the one who got him running. He was a swimmer and water polo player, definitely not a runner, and in the beginning he'd ride his bike alongside me sometimes, keeping me company and pushing my pace. It wasn't until sophomore year that he started running with me on the weekends because his coach said he needed the conditioning—and because it was another way to spend time together with how busy our schedules had gotten. We'd meet up in the early mornings between our houses like this for a run into town, have a huge breakfast at Lucille's, then walk back home the long way, talking and laughing like we had all the time in the world.

I stop, chest all of a sudden aching, out of breath. "I don't think I can—"

My dad turns around. "You okay?"

"No—I—I think I need to go back."

Ryan stops and turns. Her cheeks are flushed, and she's breathing hard as she walks back to me. I expect her to give me an order to keep running, but her eyes soften when she looks at me. "You're okay," she says. "It's just your first time back out here. You don't need to go back."

Dad seems to understand too. "Come on. Let's do this together. We'll go easy."

"Just focus on breathing," Ryan says. "Let your legs do the rest."

She turns and starts up again, and this time my dad motions for me to go in front of him. I take a step, and then another and another, until I've fallen into a semblance of a rhythm, albeit one that feels heavy and out of practice. And after a few minutes we settle into a slow but steady pace. Ryan pulls me forward, and the rhythm of one foot in front of the other gets a little easier. I breathe hard, in-out, in-out, in-out, and my heart pounds away, unused to working like this. My legs burn at first, then start to itch as blood fills and expands the capillaries in a way that it hasn't for so long. My body starts to remember, starts to come back. Starts to wake up again, like yesterday.

Ryan turns off onto a single-track dirt trail, and I know right away where we're going. I look back at Dad, and his smile says he does too.

"The ridge?" I yell up to Ryan. "On the first run back?"

"Yep," she calls over her shoulder. "No sense half stepping!"

"You're trying to kill me," I yell.

"I'm trying to do the opposite," she says. "You got this."

The three of us weave our way through the oaks at the base of the hill, where the shade makes it a touch cooler than is comfortable, and I do my best to keep up. In spite of the hard work, I start to relax a little, stop thinking so much. The morning smell of the plants and the night-cooled dirt rises up all around, and I breathe it in.

After a mile or so of rolling hills, the trail takes a hard turn and makes a steep climb up a series of switchbacks, and the only thing in my mind then is making it to the top without walking, because as we all used to say on the team, there's no walking in running. Ryan stays one turn ahead of me, so I only catch little glimpses of her as she takes on the hill. Behind me my dad's breathing becomes more labored, just as mine does, and I keep glancing over my shoulder, checking to see if he's okay.

"You doing all right?" I ask over my shoulder.

"Hanging in there," he puffs. "You?"

"Same."

We don't say anything else as our focus shifts to making it up the hill. Just when I think I may have to break the cardinal rule of running, the trail begins to level out, and the trees open up to a view of the cloudless sky first, then the tops of other hills, and finally, the ocean.

Ryan's already sitting on the giant boulder that is our destination, looking flushed and triumphant. She stands when she sees us, puts her hands to her mouth, and lets out a whoop. Dad catches up to me and puts his arms up in the air like he's crossing a finish line. I do too, because it really does feels like an accomplishment.

"Nicely done," Ryan says, reaching down a hand to help me onto the rock. "I knew you guys would make it all the way to the top."

"I didn't," I say, hoisting myself up.

Dad grabs hold of the rock and pulls himself up too, and we all stand there at the top of the ridge, looking over miles that separate our golden hills from the variegated blues of the ocean and the sky.

"Look at it," Ryan says as we catch our breaths. "It feels so faraway, but really it's right there." She looks at me then. "You just have to see it—what's in front of you. The forest for the trees, or the ocean over the hills."

"Tell us more, O wise Ryan," Dad says, still out of breath but clearly amused. When did you get so philosophical?"

Ryan rolls her eyes and nudges him with her elbow. "Last quarter, in philosophy." Then she turns to us both. "Or . . ." She pauses and looks down at her feet for a moment, then back at our dad. "Either that, or a few days ago, when Ethan broke up with me at the airport," she says flatly.

"What?" I can't contain my shock.

"Ouch," Dad says, wincing for her. "I'm sorry, sweetheart. That must've stung."

"Yeah. But only for a day or two." She kicks a pebble off the rock, and we all watch as it tumbles down the ridge. "I'm done with that now."

"Are you?" Dad asks.

"I'm working on it. . . ."

I'm still trying to process that someone broke up with my sister. No one's ever broken up with my sister.

"Atta girl," he says. "That's all you can do." He wraps an arm around her shoulder. "I never liked that guy anyway. Kind of a douche."

That makes her laugh.

Dad puts a hand on Ryan's back. "You want me to find him? Knock him down a peg or two?"

"No, I kind of already did, I think." A slow smile spreads over her face.

Dad raises his eyebrows. "Oh yeah?"

"What did you do?" I can see my sister, angry, in the middle of an airport, and the possibilities are endless.

"The details aren't really important. Let's just say I was escorted out of the boarding area by some nice men with walkie-talkies who were very concerned about where one of my shoes was, but not enough to let me go back and get it."

"You threw your *shoe* at him?" I ask, even though I'm sure she did.

"Among other things—my Starbucks, my phone . . ." She shrugs. Lets out a puff of breath. "I'm just glad I didn't make it all the way to Europe before I found out what an ass he was."

"There you go," my dad says. "Live and learn."

"Exactly," Ryan says. She looks at me then, and I know as soon as she says the words that she's not talking about herself anymore.

"And then you move forward."

"Write it on your heart that every day is the best day in the year. No man has learned anything rightly, until he know that every day is Doomsday."

—Ralph Waldo Emerson

CHAPTER SIXTEEN

I DON'T KNOW how to answer Colton's texts. I pace my room, full of more energy than I've had in a long time, then grab my phone and sit down on my floor and read them again. What do I say? Was it really an invitation to hang out? What time does "later" mean?

I need help with this, so I get back up and cross the hall to Ryan's room. When I poke my head in, I can hear her shower, so I tiptoe in. Take a look around at what was a neat and orderly room just a few days ago. Now her bags lie in the corner spilling clothes and makeup. Books and magazines litter both sides of the bed, and she's even pulled out all her old canvases from the closet and leaned them against the wall like a minigallery, and I know as soon as I see them she really is serious about putting together a portfolio for that art school.

My eyes fall on the dresser, the one neat spot, where

Ryan's completed vision board now sits leaning against the mirror, an artful, color-filled collage of her wants and goals. Of her plans to move forward. She must've stayed up into the wee hours of the morning to finish it. Either that, or she never went to bed. She has that kind of manic focus about her, like if she just keeps moving, the things she's upset about can't catch her. The opposite of me. It makes me wonder whether, if she hadn't been away at school this last year, it might've been different for me. More like today.

In big, bold letters across Ryan's board are the words *New Beginnings*, and below those, scattered over various pictures of places she wants to go, *Italy included*. Over all the images are words that sound like things my sister would say: *Get gloriously lost, find yourself, trust, love, hold your breath and take a leap*—all the things I think of her doing naturally.

I remember the one picture I found, of the heart in the bottle. I stashed the magazine under the bed, hoping she wouldn't find the picture and cut it out for herself. When I crouch down and look, it's still there. In her bathroom, the shower shuts off and I flip through fast. Find the dog-eared page opposite the picture of the heart in the bottle and slip out of Ryan's room with the magazine. Not that she'd care. She'd probably even send me off with the stack of magazines to finish my own board. But something about this particular picture makes me want to keep it to myself.

In my room, I sit down in the bright square of sunshine

on the carpet. I open the magazine to the page and carefully cut out the picture, holding it there a moment. I'm not sure of what it represents for me—only that it feels like something I need.

I go to my own dresser mirror, where the pictures of me and Trent are tucked all around the edges, and the dried sunflower from that first day we met hangs from the top corner. I don't take any of them down like Ryan seems so set on me doing. I'm not ready for that, not yet.

Instead I slide the picture between the mirror and its frame. Front and center. And then I let my eyes fall on the sunflower that Colton gave me just two days ago. It lies on top of my dresser, the petals still deep gold, with just a hint of wilt along the edges from not being put in any water. I pick it up and twirl the stem between my thumb and forefinger, setting the flower spinning into a bright blur before I go to my bookshelf and find the glass bowl left over from Ryan's graduation-party centerpieces, with their flower petals and floating candles.

I take the bowl to my bathroom sink, rinse and fill it, then come back to my dresser and the flower. The stem is thick, and it takes a few tries to cut through it with the scissors; but I cut it off close to the base of the flower, and once the flower's free I set it in the small glass bowl of water. It floats there, bright, and alive, and brave in its own little sea beneath the picture. Like I felt on the ocean.

Like I want to feel again.

Before I can talk myself out of it, I'm in the car. On the passenger seat is my bag, packed again for a day at the beach, and again it's mostly a pretense. In my pocket is money from my dad for lunch and my kayak lesson. I tried to leave without taking it because doing so felt like such a lie, but he wouldn't let me out the door without it. He, like Mom and Ryan, seems to share the hope that this will be the magic thing for me, and now I feel a responsibility at least to pretend it is.

It's still relatively early when I head down the driveway and pull onto the road. I roll down the windows and breathe in the air and the already-heavy heat coming off the hills. As soon as I hit the highway, the air rushes past, fresh and cooler, and it feels like I'm dipping a toe back into the flow of life that's been going on without me this whole time. I have no plan, and I don't know what I'm going to say when I get there, but I do like Colton told me yesterday and dive in without thinking about it.

The momentum is enough to carry me down the winding road to Shelter Cove, past the bluff where Colton and I were just yesterday, and onto the little main street, where right away my eyes find his turquoise bus parked in front of his family's shop. This time there is no open spot near it, or anywhere on the street, so I drive all the way to the parking lot at the base of the pier, and I park there. It isn't until I shut off the car and sit in the quiet a moment that I really think about what it is I'm doing here.

The rush of energy I felt when I left the house fades out like the end of a song, and there's a gnawing guilt left in its place. I do know what I'm doing. I'm using my half-truth about the kayak lesson, and Colton's texts, as reasons to be back here. But they're more like excuses—to forget my own rules, to ignore the tug of my conscience. To see him again. All these things I want are so much stronger than my rules and reasons. Strong enough that they bring me right back to his shop, where I can see the kayaks all lined up in their racks and silhouettes moving behind the window.

My stomach flutters and I stop midstep, almost turn around, but then I see a flash of his profile. He's carrying a stack of life jackets, but as his eyes sweep over the street out the window, he stops. I know he sees me, because he smiles right at me. And now it's too late to turn around. I swallow down all the butterflies that have taken flight in my stomach and force my feet to move.

He's out the doorway in less than a second, shaking his head like he can *and* can't believe I'm standing there. "You're here," he says, unable to keep his smile from spreading over his whole face, right up to the green of his eyes. He holds his hands out wide at his sides. "Here it is, another day and . . . ," he pauses, "here *you* are."

The breeze lifts a few stray strands of my hair around my face, sending chills down the back of my neck. Colton takes a step toward me and lifts his hand like he might brush them away, but he pauses, just barely, and runs his hand through the waves of his own brown hair instead. "That's unexpected," he says.

"I hope it's okay; I—"

Before I can finish, a cute blond girl who looks vaguely familiar steps out of the shop. "Hey, Colt, can you get the—"

She stops short when she sees me, looks from me to Colton and back again. "Oh hi. I'm sorry. I didn't know there was anyone else out here. Can I help you with something?" Her tone is friendly and helpful, like I'm a customer.

My stomach drops, and I stand there without saying anything for a moment. This is Shelby. The Shelby whose words and thoughts I've read. Whose joys and fears I've seen. Who I feel like I know, maybe even better than Colton.

My conscience comes rushing back at me, the full weight of all my rules and the reasons I've broken them behind it.

"I was actually just going," I say quickly. Meeting Colton

was one thing, but this is a line I didn't even anticipate crossing.

"Wait—what about kayaking?" Colton says, like it's something we were in the middle of discussing. His eyes catch mine for a tiny moment, and something flickers through them.

"I, um . . . I changed my mind." My mouth goes dry, and I take a step back. "Maybe another day? I didn't mean to bother you at work."

"Wait," Colton says again. "You're not—it's fine. I was off work a half hour ago."

Shelby laughs at this. "Wait—all that aimless pacing earlier was work?"

Colton shoots her a look, then turns his eyes back to me. "Quinn, this is my little big sister, Shelby. Shelby, my friend Quinn. She had her first kayak experience yesterday, and now she's back for more. Think we might head over to the caves again."

Shelby raises an eyebrow at Colton, then smiles and reaches out her hand "Always nice to meet a friend of Colton's," she says, a hint of something in her voice. It's the same tone I got from the nurses at the hospital at first, and I deserve it. She gives me a quick smile, then turns back to Colton.

"That's awesome, but you're booked already, Colt." I can hear it in her voice. She doesn't want him to go anywhere with me.

"Booked?" Colton laughs. "I'm not *booked*. I'm not even allowed—"

Shelby gives him a look. "Exactly."

"C'mon," he says, stepping toward her. His eyes plead, and there's something in his voice that sounds like it has to do with more than just me.

She puts up a hand. "Don't. Mom and Dad would kill me—you know that." Her eyes, level and serious, stay on his.

Colton sighs, exasperated, then seems to remember me and smiles, but this time it's tighter, more for show. "Dad's not here, Shel. And besides, she's not a customer, she's a friend."

"Colton, I can't *because* they're not here. And he left me in charge. And if something happened—"

"Nothing's gonna happen. We won't take a shop kayak. I'll take Dad's—it's in the back."

Shelby heaves a heavy sigh and chews her bottom lip, clearly debating. "That's not the point."

"Then what is?" Colton says, with more force behind his voice than I've heard him use yet. "It'll be fine. *I'm* fine." He brings his hand to his chest for a moment, which maybe wouldn't be a noticeable thing for anyone else, but I understand it and so does she.

"Colton—" There's a waver in her voice, like she's torn.

"Say yes," he says, flashing a dimpled smile. "Please.

Quinn wants to kayak, she's a beginner, and it wouldn't be right to let her go alone. Dad would be pissed if we did and he found out about *that*."

Shelby looks at Colton for a moment longer, and I can see her reluctance turn to resignation, and it makes me think of the post she wrote about Colton's first time back out on the water, and how proud and happy he was to be back doing what he loved, even though it made her whole family nervous.

"Fine," she says after a long moment. "But you have to be back in a few hours. I have a four-person tour at three o'clock, and you really do have an appointment." She holds his eyes for a long moment. "Don't forget your—"

"Got it," Colton cuts her off.

"And make sure you take your phone with you," she adds, "and if anything happens—"

He wraps an arm around her shoulders and gives her a squeeze. "We'll be fine, I promise. Right?" He looks at me, and all of a sudden I feel this big sense of responsibility. This is his sister I'm talking to, the one who's been with him and supported him and helped take care of him all along. Who worries about him more in the way a mom would than a sibling.

I glance at Shelby, asking for some kind of approval, but the smile she gives me doesn't seem to grant it.

"Right," I say finally, and the word feels heavy on

my tongue. Laden, somehow, with responsibility and the knowledge that I've just sunk myself in even deeper.

Colton claps his hands. "Good. I'm gonna pull around back to load the boat up, and I'll meet you out front in a minute."

"Okay." I nod. "I'll just . . . I'll go get my bag." I turn to head back to my car, not wanting to stand there alone with Shelby, but she stops me with a gentle hand on my arm.

She glances down at the stitches in my lip. "You're the girl Colton took to the hospital the other day?"

My heart pounds in my chest under her direct look. "Yes."

"Be careful," she says, looking me right in the eye. "Those aren't supposed to get wet."

I know she's talking about the stitches, but I can't help but hear the echo of the nurse's *be careful* when she says the words. I nod like I would to my mom telling me something.

"I will." I take a step back. "It was nice to meet you."

"You too." She smiles but doesn't go back in the shop.

I turn and cross the street, trying not to look like I'm hurrying off, and picturing her watching me the whole way. When I reach my car, I chance a tiny, sidelong glance back and she waves. Message received. Loud and clear. I open the door and run through the whole exchange in my head—her worry, his insistence that he's okay, what he's not allowed to do—and it makes me nervous. Is he not okay?

Shelby hasn't posted anything for a long time, so I don't know if there's anything to be worried about medically. . . .

What am I doing, what am I doing, what am I—

I hear the idle of an engine at my back and know it's Colton in his bus, with the kayak loaded on top and his sister's concern and my promise to be careful trailing after him. "That was fast," I say.

"We gotta get out of here before she changes her mind," he says, smiling through the open window. "Get in."

And once again, in spite of all the voices in my mind that say *don't*, that there's too much at stake, that it's not fair to Colton, and that I don't know what I'm doing, I listen to the tiny, soft voice that comes from somewhere deeper, the one that insists that maybe I do.

"Nobody has ever measured, not even poets, how much a heart can hold."

—*Zelda Fitzgerald*

CHAPTER SEVENTEEN

WE STAND AT the edge of the bluff, looking at the waves that thunder down onto the rocks with a force I can feel in my chest. "Um. I don't . . ." I shake my head, this time choosing the voice of logic and self-preservation.

"Kayaking may not be in the cards after all," Colton says. We watch as another wave pounds and swirls over the rocks that seemed so peaceful yesterday, and I couldn't agree more. "I've got a better idea," he says. "C'mon."

We hop back into his bus, and I settle into the cracked vinyl of the seat, getting used to the feel of it beneath my legs. Colton twists to see over his shoulder as he backs up, and puts an arm on the back of my headrest, his fingers just barely brushing my shoulder. It sends a little shiver through me, one he sees when our eyes catch as he turns and takes his arm away.

Heat blooms in my cheeks, and I laugh.

"What?" Colton asks.

"Nothing." I shake my head and look out the windshield, over the dashboard, behind us, where a surfboard lies on the bed, down to the sandy floorboards beneath my feet—anything not to look at him right then, because I'm afraid of what he might see on my face. When I glance down, something catches my eye. It's a clear pill counter box like my mom sets up for my dad every morning with his medications and a whole slew of vitamins. This one has two rows, every box has at least one pill in it, and instead of the letters for the days of the week, there are times written on them in Sharpie.

The question is on my tongue when Colton sees what I'm looking at. He reaches over and scoops up the box, tucking it into the pocket of his door with a tight smile. "Vitamins," he says. "Sister's big on them. Sends them with me everywhere." Something in his tone, and the way he looks back at the road right away, warns me not to ask any questions, but I don't need to. I know they're not vitamins.

We zip along the coast highway, windows down so our hair blows wild around our faces, music turned up loud so no words are necessary, and it feels good. We leave that tense moment behind.

"So where are we going?" I ask over the music.

The highway makes a wide arc inland, and we take the exit. Colton turns the music down a couple of notches.

"Another one of my favorite places," he says. "But first we need some provisions."

We pull into the dusty parking lot of the Riley Family Fruit Barn, a place my family and I used to come every fall to pick apples and take pictures with the mountains of brightly colored pumpkins every different shade of orange imaginable. I've never been here in the summertime, but clearly I've been missing out. The parking lot is crowded with families—getting in and out of cars, unpacking strollers, loading full baskets of produce into their trunks. A tractor pulling a flatbed trundles by, packed with kids and parents, some holding full, round watermelons and others taking bright juicy bites from fresh-cut wedges.

I follow Colton as he weaves among the people and into the shade of the produce stand. He brushes his fingers absently over the rainbow of fruits as he goes. "Best place ever to pick a picnic," he says over his shoulder, tossing me a peach I barely catch.

"What do you like?" Colton says, stopping in front of a display holding multitiered stacks of perfect produce. I scan it and spot a basket of raspberries so red they don't look real. Colton swoops them up. "What else? Sandwiches? Chips? Everything?"

"Yes." I laugh. "Everything, why not?"

He's so happy about it all, it's contagious.

We load up a basket full of picnic supplies—a couple of sandwiches, chips, old-fashioned sodas in glass bottles, more fruit—and then top it off with the honey sticks in the canisters next to the register. Two of every flavor.

Outside, three friendly minigoats trail behind us with hungry eyes and silly little grunts as we walk. Being next to Colton like this, in the sunshine and the coastal air, I feel the lightness of the day. Easy. Like we've left our real worlds far away. We find a bench in the shade and sit, side by side, sharing the raspberries straight out of the basket and tossing a few to the goats who now sit in front of us begging. He tells me some story of how he was traumatized by these same goats as a kid, and I laugh and lean into him, and for a second I forget myself and let a hand fall on his leg like the familiar gesture that it is.

He stops midsentence and glances down just as I take it away. There's a long moment of quiet. I try and think of something to say. Colton checks his watch. Clears his throat.

"So I have someplace I want to show you, but we need to go soon so I can get back in time for my sister not to freak out," he says, standing up. "You might want to make a restroom stop before we go—there isn't really one where we're headed."

"Okay." I stand quickly, thankful for an excuse to take

a moment to get myself together. He points at a sign with the silhouette of a farm girl on it, and I start that way. "Be right back."

"I'll be here," he says, opening a bottle of water.

I cross the parking lot to the restroom and glance back, just for a second, but it's long enough to see him open his door, pull out the pill counter, shake a few pills out, and wash them down with a swallow of water.

I feel for him in that moment—feel for him that he has to take whatever medication it is, and feel for him that it's something he thinks he needs to hide—that any of it is something he feels he needs to hide. But I'm hiding things too. It hits me then, why it's so easy to be around him, and why maybe it's the same for him with me: we don't have to acknowledge those things we want to keep hidden. Those things that define us to those who know us. We can be remade, without any loss or sickness. New to each other, and to ourselves.

When I get back from the bathroom, Colton is just getting off the phone. He smiles. "Ready?" As soon as I say yes, we're in the bus again. He pulls out of the fruit barn and turns onto the road, but we don't head back to the highway. Instead we follow the road as it winds between the oak and elm trees that tower and bend until they meet above us, forming a green canopy. We drive along the curve of the hills, and when I can smell the ocean on the air, we make a sharp turn up a steep, winding road, climbing at an almost impossible angle.

"Where are we going?" I ask again.

"You'll see," Colton says. "We're almost there."

When we finally reach the crest of the hill, I can see we're on a point, far above the ocean that surrounds us on three sides, deep blue and sparkling like the sun spilled out and broke into tiny pieces over its surface. We park in a little dirt patch on the side of the road, and Colton glances at my feet in their flip-flops. "You okay to do a little hike in those? It's not far."

"Sure."

"Good." He smiles. "Because I think you'll like this place.

I look around, and all of a sudden I know where we are. "Is this Pirate's Cove? That nude beach?" I'd heard of it before, heard that it was full of nothing but old, over-weight, naked men who sometimes played volleyball and always laid out and tanned, well, everything. "Are we—we're not going *there*, are we?"

Colton laughs so hard he spits out the sip of water he just took. When he finally gets ahold of himself, he smiles at me. "No, we're not going for a picnic at Pirate's Cove—unless of course you really want to. Where we're going has a way better view than that. Follow me."

He grabs the bag with all our picnic supplies in it and puts the loops over his shoulder, then heads for a little dirt trail I hadn't noticed when we parked. I'm still standing in the same spot when Colton turns around. "You coming?"

I follow him down the narrow trail that twists through shrubs so high it feels like we're in a tunnel, and the only thing I can see is him in front of me. We don't talk, and I can't help but wonder what it is we're going to see, but I don't ask. I like the idea of not knowing, and the sense that wherever he's taking me will give me another little glimpse into him. After a few minutes he slows his pace and so do I, until he stops completely.

"Okay, you ready?"

"For what?"

"For my favorite lunch spot."

"Ready."

He steps aside, and in front of us is a cave that opens out to the ocean like a window. Through it, I can see the deep blue of the water and the wide span of the horizon, and I realize it's one of the places he told me about while we were lying on the beach. And we're here, just like he said we'd be.

"Come on," he says, taking my hand. "Just watch for glass in the cave. People leave a lot behind."

It's noticeably cooler when we step into the arch of rock, but what I feel more than anything is the heat of Colton's hand around mine as we make our way over the remnants of secret parties and hidden bonfires on summer nights. When we get to the other side, where the sunlight and ocean sounds pour in, he drops his hand.

"What do you think? Not a bad view, right?"

"Not at all," I manage.

The edge of the cliff we're on is like the edge of the world, with its sheer drop below us. Colton lowers himself and sits, dangling his feet over it like he would if he were sitting on any chair or bench anywhere else. I inch down to the ground and do the same thing, though it makes my heart skip more than a beat. He brushes off a little space between us and unpacks our picnic, and soon enough we've got our backs leaned into the rock on one side of the cave and a breeze blowing over us as we take in the view. Colton picks up his sandwich, but instead of taking a bite, he looks over the water like he's thinking about something. "Do you know what's really strange?" he asks, after a wave crashes and recedes.

"What?"

"It's strange that I don't know you at all, not really." He pauses. "But I know a lot *about* you."

I'm glad he's not looking at me, because I'm sure I must go pale. If only he knew how strange it really is. How much I know about him without actually knowing him either. How many pictures I've seen, how many moments of his life, big and happy and painful and scary. Moments that moved me to tears, made me want to know him, justified my finding him.

And then I think of how well I know the heart that beats in his chest right now. How knowing it makes me feel like I know him on another level too. How a tiny little part of me wonders if Trent's heart in his chest is what makes it so easy to be with Colton. Is what gives us that feeling, like maybe even though we don't know each other that well, our hearts do.

"Hm" is all I say—is all I *can* say. I take a small bite of my sandwich so I don't have to add anything, even though I have no appetite at the moment. Something about his tone makes me scared to go down the path of this conversation with him, but I can't help it.

"What . . . do you know?" I ask, despite my fear of what his answer will be.

"Well, for starters, I know you're not the world's best driver," he says with a grin.

"Funny."

"Let's see," he says, like he's thinking. "I know you live in the country with a family you're close to."

I nod.

"That you have one dimple when you smile, and that you should smile more because I like it."

This makes me smile.

"See?" he says. "Like that."

Heat creeps from my chest up my neck.

"I know you're brave about doing things that scare you. Like the kayak yesterday, or sitting here right now." He looks me in the eye. "I like that too."

His eyes roam over my face for a moment that feels too long, but then they come back to mine, and he speaks softer, gentler. "You trust easy, but questions seem like they scare you, which means . . ." He pauses, seems to be weighing his next words carefully. "You have things you don't want to talk about."

I look away, scared that if I let him see my face, he'll know more than he does already—that he'll see everything.

"It's okay," he says, reading my reaction wrong. "We all have stuff we carry around like that, things we'd rather just forget about." He pauses and takes in a deep breath that comes out in a heavy sigh. "Problem is, most of the time you can't. No matter how hard you try."

I hear two things in his voice right then. Pain and, beneath that, guilt. I know those feelings so well, they're not hard to recognize, and I think I might understand why he never answered my letter. It must've been everything he didn't want—a connection to his past, and the acknowledgment of a stranger's death, and the pain of those mourning that death. The guilt must've come with that.

Empathy is what I feel in this moment. Because the

things we're carrying around, that we're not talking about, they are the same.

A wave thunders down on the rocks below, and white water engulfs them, hiding them momentarily beneath swirling white foam. I look at Colton, and he reaches his hand to my face, brushes his thumb slowly across my cheek, which I realize is wet with tears again.

"I'm sorry," he says. "For whatever it is that you went through."

"Don't be," I say. It comes out with more force and emotion than I mean for it to. I want to take away the weight of his guilt. "Please don't ever be sorry." I want to make him understand what I really mean. I look at him then, and I say something Trent's mom said to me that I didn't believe. Right now I want, more than anything, for Colton to believe it for himself. "You can't be sorry for something you had no control over."

He looks down at his lap, then brings his eyes back to mine, searching like he knows there's something else there, something between us that runs deeper than this conversation, but he can't see it, and I don't show him. We're sitting on the edge of a cliff with a long fall and no safety net.

"Then let's not be sorry," he says, steering us away from it. "Let's just be here now."

"Is that, like, your mantra?"

"Sort of." He shrugs. He's about to say something else,

but his phone rings from his pocket. He reaches in and silences it.

"Do you need to answer that?"

"No, it's just my sister."

"Maybe you should get it. She seemed a little worried earlier."

"She's always like that with me," he says. "Protective."

He waves a hand like it's no big deal, but his eyes leap out to the water, avoiding mine. "She means well by it, I know, but it can be a little much. Sometimes I think she still sees me as pretty helpless."

We're quiet for a moment, and I think of the picture of him from when he first went into the hospital—pale but smiling, flexing his thin arms, Shelby standing at his side doing the same thing. I glance at him out of the corner of my eye, at the same dark hair and green eyes set off against the deep tan of his face.

"That's not what I see," I say.

"No?" he asks with a smile.

"No."

He leans in close. "Then what do you see?"

I'm aware of the shakiness of my breath, and his, as I look at him. All the pictures in my mind—the ones of him before, and the ones of Trent—disappear, and I am here with Colton, now.

"I see . . ." I pause and lean back a little, putting more

space between us. "I see someone who's strong. Who knows a lot about life already. Someone who understands what it means to take a day and make it a good one." I pause, looking down at the water for a moment, then back at him. "Someone who's teaching me to do the same." I smile. "I like that."

This makes him smile.

"So maybe we could keep doing this," I say, surprising myself. "Making each day better than the last, and being here now, and all of that."

"Tomorrow?"

"Or the next day."

"Both."

His phone beeps again. "Damn," he says. "We need to go."

Another wave crashes on the rocks far below, sending its salty mist swirling up and around us, blurring our pasts and the things we don't want to think about. We linger there in the present moment and the possibilities it holds for a few more minutes, and then we collect our things and go back to our separate worlds.

"You will need to take anti-rejection medicines for the life of your [heart] transplant. It's vital that you never stop taking your anti-rejection medicines, or change the dose, unless your transplant doctor or nurse tells you to do so. Stopping your anti-rejection medications will eventually allow your body to reject the organ."
—University of Chicago Hospital Patient Care Guide, "Life after Your Transplant"

CHAPTER EIGHTEEN

RYAN'S CAR IS the only one in the driveway when I get back. When I walk up the porch steps, I can see her lying out next to the pool on one of the lounge chairs, one of Mom's cooking magazines draped over her face. I walk over, not sure if she's awake, and she lifts the corner slightly when she hears me.

"Hey, how was the kayak lesson?"

It's a normal question, but I can hear the smile in her voice, like she's joking by asking it. Testing me out.

I sit on the lounge chair next to her. "The waves were too big to go out today."

"So what'd you do instead?"

"Came back here."

She takes the magazine from her face, then reaches back and reties her top before she sits up. "Yeah, but you were gone all day. What'd you do *before* you came back?"

"We—I—" I catch myself too late.

"Ha. I knew it." She raises an eyebrow and smiles. "So who is he?"

"What if I was with one of my friends?"

Ryan lowers her sunglasses and levels her eyes at me. "When's the last time you hung out with any of your friends?"

I shrug. I really can't remember.

"Right. So who's the guy?"

"How do you know there is one? "

"Wild guess," she says. "That, and I can tell when you're not telling me something. So talk. Who is he?"

I don't answer right away. I want to tell her about Colton, and the day. I want to tell her how it felt sitting next to him on that cliff. That I'm worried and drawn in at the same time. I want her to give me advice, like she did the first time I asked about kissing Trent, and after the first fight we had, and whether or not I should be the first one to say I love you, or if I was ready to sleep with him. Ryan always had the answer to all my questions.

I want to know what she would think if she knew the truth, but I'm terrified of it too.

"He's," I say, choosing my words—and details—carefully, "he's the kayak instructor who gave me the lesson the other day. We just had lunch today—since we couldn't take the kayak out." Half-truths, omissions.

"Aaannd . . ." She leans in, waiting.

"And then I came home."

The latest issue of *Eating Well* comes flying at me and I have to duck. "Oh come on. Tell me *something*."

"I did."

She gives me a look.

"His name's Colton."

Ryan motions like *Come on*, and I so badly want to tell her more.

Instead I shrug. "I don't know, he's . . . he's really sweet, and we just hung out."

"That's great," she says, reaching a hand out to my leg. She pats it. "It really is. It's a good thing to be moving forward."

Moving forward sounds better than moving on, but I'm still hit by a pang of guilt at the thought, which must somehow show on my face, because Ryan changes the subject.

"Anyway, it's better than I can say for myself at the moment." She gestures at the magazines and candy wrappers spread all around her. "Does he happen to have a sweet older brother?"

"Just a sister," I say before I can stop myself. I ask a quick question to avoid any more from her. "Are you okay? You seem . . ."

Ryan shrugs. "Bored? I am. I was supposed to be on the other side of the world right now, but here I am. Back home. Lying by the pool, reading Mom's magazines, hanging out with Gran and her Red Hat ladies. I love them and all, but their lives are more exciting than mine right now, which is just . . . sad."

"What about your whole vision-board thing, and your art portfolio? What about the run today? I thought you were all ready for new beginnings, and conquering the world."

Ryan rolls her eyes. "I know. That's called faking it until you make it." She purses her lips a second. "Clearly I haven't made it yet."

"What do you mean?"

"I mean Ethan dumped me in the middle of the airport and flew off to Europe alone, and I'm so . . ." She shakes her head, and I know she's replaying whatever happened in her mind, and I'm sure she's about to get angry all over again, but she looks at the ground, and her shoulders just kind of sag.

"I'm so sad."

It's like it appears on her face instantly now that she's said it, and I can't believe I didn't see it until this second.

"I was so in love with him." Her eyes fall to her lap. "*Am* so in love with him." She shakes her head again. "And I *hate* it, because he took my heart and just stomped all over it. I shouldn't love him still. And now . . . it's like this paralyzing kind of feeling. Like my world just crumbled right in front of me, you know?"

I nod. I do, more than anyone.

"Oh Jesus, I'm sorry. That was a stupid thing to say."

"No it wasn't," I say. "It not like . . . it's not like it just happened. You don't have to keep being so careful around me. Actually, I kinda like the whole 'fake it till you make it' approach. That run hurt, but it felt good too, to be out there again."

"Yeah, it did," Ryan agrees, but she still looks a little lost.

"So maybe we can just keep faking it together for a little while? Keep running?"

Ryan thinks about it for a moment, and the spark comes back into her eyes. "Yeah, I like that. But first we need to get out of this house. And get us some more chocolate. And maybe some new running clothes, if we're gonna fake it right. Your ratty old running shorts aren't gonna fool anyone."

I toss the magazine back at her. "That's my favorite pair. I've had them forever."

"Yeah, well in the interest of moving forward, it's time you found a new favorite pair of shorts."

We make the drive into town, with Ryan behind the wheel, which is always somewhere between fun and terrifying.

With the music blasting loud and my sister singing next to me, it feels like it used to. Almost like it used to—but better, closer, like we're in this together. We hit Target, the one major store in town, just like we used to before Ryan left for college, grab a coffee at Starbucks, and cruise the air-conditioned aisles for the things we need and don't need. By the time I come home, I've got a whole new running wardrobe, courtesy of Ryan and her leftover travel money.

Up in my room, I take everything out of the bags and lay it out on the bed, feeling motivated by my new gear just like Ryan said I would. I check my phone for the fiftieth time, but there are no texts from Colton. It's not quite dinner yet, and I have a little time to kill, so I cross the room to my desk, flip open my laptop, and click over to Shelby's blog, hoping for something new, some new picture of him, or a little quote or story about him, but it's the same post that's been up since his one-year checkup.

> To all our friends and family, we are so thankful for all your support. It's been a long year, but Colton's checkup came back great, and he's finally adjusting to all his meds. . . .

I remember the pill box, and Colton swallowing the pills when he thought I couldn't see him. I sit there for a moment, then type into the search box "Post–heart transplant medications."

Millions of results come up in seconds, lots from medical journals and articles that I don't think I'll understand, but lower on the results page, a line from some sort of transplant message board catches my eye:

> "You've traded in death for a lifetime of medical management. . . ."

I click on the link to the quote, which comes from a forty-two-year-old heart transplant patient. He continues:

> Don't get me wrong—I'd make that trade again in a second. And at my age, that's something I can handle. There are limitations. Medical limitations, and physical ones too. Risks that you take when you're young and *don't* have a medical condition. Much as you want to, that's not something you can forget. You can't afford to. Doesn't matter if you're tired, or you don't want to take them because you hate the way they make you feel. Doesn't matter if there are major side effects. That's a part of your life now, just like checkups, and biopsies, and monitoring your weight, blood pressure, heart rate. It's a gift, but a huge responsibility to shoulder. And if you can't find a way to get on board with all that, then you're risking yourself and your transplant. You have to be careful with yourself, and honest about your limits.

I think of Colton. How healthy he seems. And strong. But maybe there are limitations I can't see, or don't know about. It makes me want to be careful with him—like the nurse said, like Shelby said without actually saying those words. It makes me feel responsible for his heart, in more ways than one.

"The rhythms that count—the rhythms of life, the rhythms of the spirit—are those that dance and course in life itself. The movement in gestation from conception to birth; the diastole and systole of the heart; the taking of each successive breath; the ebb and flow of tides in response to the pull of the moon and the sun; the wheeling of the seasons from one equinox or one solstice to another—these, not the eternally passing seconds registered on clocks and watches and not the days and months and years that the calendar imposes, define the time . . . we dwell within until our days our ended."

—*Allen Lacy,* The Inviting Garden: Gardening for the Senses, Mind, and Spirit

CHAPTER NINETEEN

AFTER THAT FIRST morning run, Ryan and I take turns choosing our running route. It's busy at the office, more than Mom can handle on her own, so Dad is back to his normal routine and it's just the two of us. We run down roads lined with row after row of rolling vineyards, down single-track trails into ravines with narrow creeks hidden beneath ferns and poison ivy. Sometimes we talk, but mostly it's just us, and the morning, the rhythm of our feet, and breath, and heartbeats, and the burning of my muscles and lungs as they remember how to be alive.

After our runs, Ryan heads to Gran's to paint and work on her portfolio, and I make the drive over to the coast. Somewhere along the road that twists and curves between the trees, I become the me who Colton knows.

We start meeting every day at the bluff where we went out kayaking that first day, and I wonder if it's to avoid Shelby. If he's keeping me a secret like I've kept him. I try not to think about it, and it's easy when we're together. He shows me every place he used to know, hidden coves and coastal roads, places that hold memories from his childhood. This is how I start to know him. I don't have to ask any questions, because he shows me his past this way—the past he wants me to know, without any hospital beds, or oxygen tubes, or plastic boxes full of pills.

I start to recognize the rhythm of our days—how there seem to be windows of time we can be out on the water, or under the sun. I try to be careful, try to see any limitations he might have. Our only one seems to be when he needs to take his meds. I try to anticipate it. When I think the time is coming for him to take a dose, I make sure to busy myself with whatever distraction I can find: wildflowers growing along a trail, a line of pelicans gliding low over the surface of the ocean, searching for shells in the sand. I try to give him a few moments to himself for those things he doesn't want me to see.

I learn from him all the things he does want me to see in the details he points out and in the things he says. I learn that he admires his dad but that he is closest to his grandfather, who passed on his love of the sea and all its old sailors' legends. He knows just about every constellation in the sky and the stories behind all of them. He really does think each day can be better than the last.

I think he learns from me, too. I let things come out without him having to ask. I tell him about running with Ryan, and about Gran and her Red Hat ladies. I tell him I'm not sure what comes next for me. That I like what we're doing now. That I want to keep doing this.

And there's this current running between us, building and growing in our quiet moments, and in the laugh-out-loud ones too. I see it when our eyes catch and he smiles, hear it in the way he says my name. I feel it whenever our hands or shoulders or legs brush up against each other. I think he does too, but there's something holding him back. I don't know if it's for my sake or his, but we dance around each other, Colton and I, despite the magnets in our centers, the full-of-life beating ones that pull us closer every day.

One day, after we've kayaked and had lunch, I tell him I want to learn how to surf, so we start in the afternoon with the basics. He pushes me into wave after wave, yelling for me to stand up and cheering each time I do—even when I fall right back down. We do this over and over until finally I get it. I paddle for a wave, as hard as I can, and I feel just a little push from him— enough to get me into it. This time when he yells for me to stand up, I do, and I find my balance and ride the wave all the way in. It's the most amazing feeling in the world, and I don't ever want to stop or get out of the water, so we stay, into the early evening, paddling out and surfing in until my arms are shaky and I can hardly lift them.

Later, we sit out beyond where the waves break, our boards floating next to each other on the glassy surface of the water. The afternoon wind has died down, and beachgoers have started to clear out, except for the ones who are staying for the sunset. The sun hangs low and heavy over the water. I can feel Colton's eyes on me as I watch it, and I turn to look at him.

"What?" I ask, feeling self-conscious.

Colton grins and swirls his foot around in the water. "Nothing, I just . . ." His face goes more serious. "Do you know how many days I spent wishing I could just do this? It's . . ."

He says something else, but I don't hear him, because one phrase is stuck in my mind. *How many days, how many days . . .*

All of a sudden I feel completely unmoored. I have no idea how many days it's been since Trent died. I don't know when I stopped counting. I don't know when I let go of that thing that grounded me in my grief, that reminded me each and every day. Like penance, for not going with him that morning, for not being with him on that road, for not being able to save him or say good-bye. And now I don't even know how many days it's been.

I lost count. Failed him again.

"Can we go in?" I say suddenly. "Please?" My chest hurts. I feel that old, familiar tightness, and I can't breathe.

"Don't you wanna wait to see if we can see it?" Colton asks.

"See what?" I ask. I've lost the thread of what he's talking about. I can't get enough air in my lungs—they're forgetting how to breathe.

"The green flash," Colton says, pointing to the sun that's now halfway disappeared below the water and sinking fast.

"The what?"

"The green flash," he says. "Watch. At that last second when the sun slips into the water, if everything is right, you can see it. Supposedly." He smiles. "My grandpa used to have us watch for it, and every time, he'd tell us this old line about how if you see the green flash, you can see into people's hearts." Colton traces a finger over the water's surface and laughs softly. "He swore he'd seen it, and that's how he always knew what everyone was thinking."

See into other people's hearts.

My heart pounds with all the truth and lies and omissions that are in it. All the things I don't want Colton to see. All the things I've been hiding from myself. I don't even know what's in my heart anymore.

"Watch," Colton says again, pointing at the horizon. "It happens fast."

We both turn back to the sun, a bright-orange ball sinking into the water that glows gold with its light. The sun does seem to accelerate, disappearing faster by the second. I panic. I want to look away; I want Colton to look away. I know it's just a story, but I hold my breath as the sun slips down, and at the last second I look at Colton. He sits still, eyes focused hard on the horizon.

And then the sun's gone.

He sighs. "No green flash tonight."

I meet his eyes for a brief moment, then look out to the empty patch of sky where the sun almost laid bare my secrets, and it's all I can do not to cry.

In my room, behind my closed door, I can't hold it back anymore. My hands shake as I take my calendar from the wall and sit down on the floor with it. How could I have lost track? Which morning did I wake up and not think the number? Which night did I go to bed without Trent being my last thought?

I flip back through the months, to day 365, which is a date I could never forget. I put my finger to the little square that comes after it, but a sob shakes me, lets loose the tears I managed to hold back all the way home. Guilt pools in my stomach.

How did I lose count?

I wipe at my eyes and try to focus on the grid of empty boxes that were days empty of Trent, days I kept track of because it was one tiny way to hold on to him, to always know how long it had been, and I need to know again—

"What are you doing?" Ryan asks. I didn't even hear her come in, but the second she sees me, she's on her knees in front of me. "What's wrong?"

I drop the calendar, put my head in my hands, and I sob.

"Quinn, hey, what's going on?" Her voice is sympathetic, which makes it even worse.

I lift my head and look at her. "I don't . . ." A fresh wave of tears comes on hard. "I don't know how many days it's been since he died, I lost count, and now I can't remember, and I need to—" I gulp for air before another sob shakes me, and I put my head back in my hands.

Ryan's arms come around me, and I feel her chin rest on my head. "Shhh . . . it's okay. It's okay," she repeats, and I want to believe her, but she has no idea. "You don't need to keep count," she says softly.

I cry into my sister's chest, the only reply I can manage.

"You don't," she says, gently pulling herself away so she can look at me. "It doesn't make it any less important, or mean that you miss him any less."

I press my lips together, shake my head. There are so many things she doesn't know.

"It doesn't," she says, firmer now. "It's going to happen, and it's supposed to happen this way. You're *allowed* to feel less pain, and you're *allowed* to feel happy again." She pauses. "You're allowed to start living again—it's not a betrayal to Trent. He'd want you to."

A fresh wave of tears springs free at his name.

"What is this about?" she asks. "Is it about forgetting the number of days, or is it about Colton? Because you've spent every day together for the last two weeks, and you know what? You've been happy. You don't need to feel guilty about that."

"But it's . . ."

"It's a *good* thing," Ryan says.

I want to believe her—and part of me does. Part of me knows she's right, because I absolutely cannot deny the way it feels to be with Colton. But I also can't deny the guilt that sits just below the surface every time I am. It seems like a betrayal to Trent to feel this way. And I know that keeping the whole thing from Colton is an even bigger betrayal. I stare at the calendar on the floor in front of me, each blank square a day that was equally as blank until I met him.

"Hey," Ryan says, squeezing my shoulder. "You're gonna have days and moments like this, when it all comes rushing back at you, and that's okay. But you're also going to have days, lots of them, when you feel good, and that's okay too." She tucks my hair behind my ear. "Believe it or not, you'll even have a day when you fall in love again. But you have to open yourself up to it."

I can tell she's trying to catch my eye, but I keep my eyes focused on the calendar in my lap.

"You two loved each other so much, but you still have a whole life to live. You have to know Trent would want that for you again."

I nod like she's right, and wipe the tears from my cheeks, and look her right in the eyes and say, "I do," but it's not because I believe her. It's because I need to be alone. Because if Trent could see me now, I don't know if he'd want me to be doing *this*.

"Your vision will become clear only when you can look into your own heart. . . . Who looks inside, awakes."

—*Carl Jung*

CHAPTER TWENTY

I'M ALREADY AWAKE when my phone buzzes from the nightstand. I know it's Colton calling to say good morning and make plans for the day, but I hesitate instead of reaching for it. I didn't explain myself after wanting to leave so abruptly yesterday, and he didn't ask, but I know this can't go on much longer—me having these mini-breakdowns and him just letting it go. Eventually, he's going to ask for some sort of explanation, and I don't know what I'll do then. The phone stops buzzing and beeps a moment later with a voicemail.

"Quinn?" There's a knock on my door. "You awake in there?" It's my dad's voice.

"I'm up," I say, loud enough for him to hear me. "Come in."

I sit up, and he opens the door but doesn't come in. He just stands there in his running clothes, which is a surprise. It's a weekday. "Morning, sunshine. Time to run."

"Where's Ryan?" I ask. After last night's episode with my calendar, I'm a little wary of seeing her as well.

"She went off to paint," Dad says, and I feel a flicker of relief. "Only has a few more days to make the deadline to submit her portfolio. She seems serious about it. Took all her stuff and said she wouldn't be back until tonight." He shrugs. "Anyway, she left me with strict orders to fill in as your running partner."

"What about work?"

"Took the day off—one of the perks of being your own boss." He claps his hands together. "Let's get goin'."

I nod, but I don't move. The calendar is still on the floor next to my bed, and I still don't know how many days it's been. After Ryan left last night, I collapsed into bed, unable to do anything, let alone count the days.

"Don't jump up all at once," he says, his face falling a little.

I immediately feel bad. "I'm sorry, I just . . ." I still feel drained after last night. Heavy and hollow at the same time. "I don't really feel like running today."

My dad comes in now and sits on the end of my bed. "What about a *breakfast* run? Now's our chance. Come on. You haven't been around much lately. I wanna hear what's new. Over bacon. And eggs. And biscuits and gravy."

"You're not allowed."

"Light gravy. Turkey bacon." He grabs my foot through

my covers. "Come on. Humor your old man with your company."

I smile and give in. I am a little hungry. And it has been a while.

We sit in the same booth we always used to when we'd come here before. Breakfast with Dad at Lucille's was another one of those things, like running, that started out as part of our regular routine, then as business picked up turned into a special occasion, and then finally just fell off altogether. I can't remember the last time we were here, but nothing about the little country diner has changed. Dad leans over his coffee in its chipped mug, closes his eyes, and breathes in the aroma like it's the best smell in the world.

"So what's new with you?" He takes a sip. Savors it. "You've become quite the beach bum these days."

I nod. "I've been having fun over there."

"And Ryan says you're getting fast again. Says you're giving her a run for her money." He takes another sip of his coffee.

"Does she?" This makes me smile, because she'd sooner push herself until she passed out than admit that to me. "That's funny, because all she says to me is that I can do better."

My dad laughs. "That sounds about right. You probably can. Your sister calls 'em like she sees 'em. Always has." He pauses and sets down his coffee to pick up his menu.

I think about the things Ryan said to me last night, about not counting the days, or feeling bad about spending time with Colton, and I want so much to believe her, but it's hard, knowing that what she sees isn't the entire picture.

My dad closes his menu and folds his hands on top of it, and I can tell there's something more to this breakfast trip. I tense, waiting to see what it is and hoping that she didn't tell him about Colton, or last night, or anything else.

"I was thinking," he says, trying to sound casual but failing. "You might want to consider signing up for a few classes over at the city college—so you could join the cross-country team. The coach there would love to have you. Said he'd gladly take you as a walk-on."

"What?" Surprise hides my relief. "You checked?"

"Ryan did."

"Wow, am I like her service project this summer?"

"No," Dad says, "she just wants to see you happy. And running again seems to be one of the things that does that for you." He pauses. "You know, along with the beach, and whoever's over there. Maybe the not-homely beach kid?"

I look down at my menu, nervous all over again. "Did Ryan tell you that too?"

"She doesn't need to—your mom and I can see it. And it's good, Quinn, it's—"

"Oh my god." I see a familiar profile stand up two booths behind my dad.

"Honey, it's really okay—"

I shake my head, motion behind him because I can't say anything.

He turns around and sees her too, only he's not paralyzed like I am at the moment. Instead he puts his napkin on the table, stands, and goes to greet Trent's mom. They hug each other, and I can't hear what they say, but I see him motion to me sitting at the table before they both come walking over. I stand, feeling guilty all of a sudden that it's been so long since I've gone to visit her.

"Quinn, honey," she says, opening her arms. "It's so good to see you!"

"You too," I say, and aside from the initial shock, it is.

She holds on so long and tight, it's a little uncomfortable. Finally, she pulls me back by my shoulders. "Look at you! You look amazing!"

"Thank you," I say. "You do too." And she does. The dark circles that seemed permanent have disappeared from beneath her eyes, and her hair has color in it again, and she's even put on makeup. She almost looks like the version of herself that used to tease us if she caught us in a kiss, and who cared about my race times as much as Trent's. Like herself, before. Almost.

"Thank you," she says. "I've been trying to get out more

these days, volunteering here and there—keeping busy. You know," she adds, and there's a hint of sadness in it.

My dad works to keep the conversation light. "Quinn has been busy too," he says. "She's running again, has taken up kayaking. . . ."

He leaves me room to jump in. I don't. "Keeping busy" seems to be code for "moving on," which seems insensitive to admit to Trent's mom, even though she said it herself first.

She tilts her head to the side, reaches out, and lays a hand on my cheek. "That is fabulous to hear, sweetheart, it really is. And what about school?"

My dad clears his throat, and I surprise myself by speaking up; but I don't want him to have to answer again for me. "I'm still figuring that one out, but I might take a few classes at the city college in the fall—enough to run for them."

I can feel my dad smile next to me.

Trent's mom throws her arms around me again. "Oh Quinn, that's just wonderful." She squeezes me tight and speaks quieter, close to my ear. "Trent would be so happy that you're doing so well. So happy."

I think of how I spent the first four hundred days after he died—for the first time, I really try to imagine what he would've thought if he could've seen me then. I don't know if it's this shift in focus or the sincerity in his mom's voice, but I believe her. I think if he could see me now, he'd want me to "keep busy," and make plans, and . . . move on.

"Listen," she says, "I have an appointment, so I need to get going, but it was so nice to see you both."

She gives me one more hug, then hugs my dad too. And then before she turns to leave, she says good-bye, but I hear something more in it. Somehow it feels a bit more final than the other good-byes we've said. More like letting go. Though it makes me a little sad, I understand it. We'll always be connected by Trent, and our past, but time has stretched that connection so it already feels weaker, which seems inevitable.

My dad looks at me after she walks out the doorway. "You okay? That was . . . unexpected."

"I'm okay," I answer honestly.

"Good," he says, wrapping his arm around my shoulder. "Shall we finish our breakfast?"

We sit back down at our table, and something in me relaxes—enough that I tell him a little about Colton: how his family owns a kayak rental shop, about the cave and how scared I was to paddle into it, and the cliff where we had a picnic. It feels good to talk about him out loud. Not to keep him so secret and separate from this part of my life. I'm on a roll with little details about all these things when I realize my dad's just smiling and listening.

"What?" I ask, all of a sudden self-conscious.

"Nothing," he says, shaking his head. "He just sounds like someone who's good to be around. Good for *you* to be around."

I smile. "He is."

I miss Colton right then, and I realize today is the first day in who knows how many that I haven't seen him. I didn't even get a chance to listen to his message.

When I get home, I close the door of my room and hit the voicemail button on my phone, waiting for Colton's voice to come on, sounding the way it always does, like he's smiling while he's talking.

"Hey, good morning. You're probably already up and running all over the hills with your sister. I know we were maybe gonna drive up the coast, but I, um, forgot I have to go up north for the day. Something for the shop, so we'll have to save that for another time. Good news is I'll be back tomorrow night, so you should definitely come down for the fireworks if you can—if you want to." He pauses. "I want you to." There's another pause, and then he laughs a little. "Anyway. Gimme a call when you can, and have a good day, okay? I'll see you tomorrow night. I hope."

I replay the message and listen to his voice a second and then a third time, and when I think of seeing him again, I hope too—that whatever it is we have can be more. That we can be more.

"There is no instinct like that of the heart."

—*Lord Byron*

CHAPTER TWENTY-ONE

IN ALL OUR days spent together, I haven't yet been to Colton's house, but he asked me to meet him here tonight. I don't have to look at the address to guess which one is his, because I see his bus parked in the open garage as soon as I turn the corner. On the stretch of bluff road that's lined with whitewashed, modern-styled houses, Colton's stands out, and my first thought is *Of course, this is his house.* It sits farther back on the property than the others, the shingled face making it look warmer and more lived-in than the surrounding houses, with their sleek lines and cold exteriors. Bright tropical flowers line the edges of the lawn, and a row of towels and wet suits hangs over the railing of the second-story deck.

I slow and park at the curb across the street, and a little wave of nervousness passes through me when I see Colton come through the doorway into the garage and throw a couple of towels into the bus. He's about to turn around and go back in when he sees me and starts in my direction. I take a deep breath before I get out, now even more anxious because it's been a day since we've seen each other and I've never been to his house before. Or maybe it's because Ryan insisted I wear her dress. Or because this is usually the time I'm heading home. It's a different feeling, arriving for the evening.

"Wow," Colton says, meeting me in the middle of his street, "you look . . . wow."

"Thanks? I think?" I say, silently thanking Ryan.

"I'm sorry, yes. That was definitely a compliment." He looks down, and I see a flash of self-consciousness in his eyes that makes me smile.

"You look wow too," I say, gesturing at his now-familiar uniform of surf T-shirt and board shorts. He laughs at this, but it's true. His shirt clings to his shoulders just enough, and the deep green of it sets off his tan and his eyes.

"Thanks," he says. "I try."

We stand there in the middle of his street, taking in the evening air and each other in the twilight, until a car comes around the corner, then slows, snapping us out of our little moment.

Colton makes a motion with his head toward his garage. "I just gotta load the kayak and then we can go." He glances over at me as we walk up the driveway. "You brought a bathing suit, right?"

"Yeah, it's in the car. Should I grab it?"

"Yeah. Actually, you may want to put it on here so you don't have to in the parking lot."

Though I'm plenty practiced at changing beneath a carefully held up towel by now, it's nice not to have to, so I go back to my car and grab my suit. When I get back to the garage, Colton's pushing the kayak onto the roof of the bus.

"Where should I . . ."

"You can use my bathroom," he says over his shoulder as he shoves the kayak forward, onto the rack above his head. "It's down the hall, last door on the left."

"Okay," I say absently, but I don't go anywhere.

My eyes have found the thin strip of skin that's exposed between the waist of Colton's board shorts and his T-shirt as he reaches up to strap the kayak onto the rack. The skin is so much lighter than his face or his arms, and I know why. He doesn't ever take off his shirt. I've never seen him with it off, have only guessed at his scars and what they look like now, always hidden beneath a wet suit or a rash guard or a shirt.

He catches me looking and smiles before his arms come down, hiding the parts of him he's not ready for me to see. "You need me to show you?"

Yes, I think. "No," I say. "I can find it." I step through the door into the hallway. Exhale.

I make the left turn and head down the hallway, which is almost dark but for a light coming through a doorway down the hall on the right. I'm about to go right past it to the bath-room door, but just as I get to the slice of light coming from the room, something on a shelf catches my eye.

I pause in front of the half-open door, not wanting to be nosy, and then glance over my shoulder to make sure Colton's not coming in too, which makes me feel even more guilty. But when I see nothing but the closed door that leads to the garage, curiosity gets the best of me and I push the door open gently.

I gasp.

Lining every wall of the room are shelves that hold bot-tles of every size and shape, and each of them contains a ship, floating in the glass. The one I saw from the hall is the biggest, like a large, clear vase on its side, with one of those tall-masted ships with sail after sail billowed out in the invisible wind. In others are smaller ships, sailboats, and other vessels whose names I don't know. Some bottles are rounded and perfectly clear; others are square, or made of thick glass, hazy with bubbles so that the ships inside have a softer, almost dreamy quality to them.

I can't help myself. I step fully into the room and pick up one of the smaller bottles. Inside this one is a pirate-looking ship, with torn dark sails that look like they're whipping around in the wind. I turn the bottle in my hands, then lift it above my head, inspecting the bottom to see if I can tell how the ship was put in.

"That one's the *Essex*," Colton says from behind. His voice sends a jolt right through me. I open my mouth to say something, fumble with the bottle in my hands, and then put it back on the shelf quickly, guilty, guilty, guilty. He takes it gently from the shelf and holds it between us.

"I'm sorry," I say. "I wasn't trying to be nosy. I was on my way to the bathroom, but then I saw the ships through the doorway, and I couldn't— Is this your room?"

Colton laughs, then sets down the bottle and scans the walls, with all their ships and bottles. "Yeah," he says.

I look around too, not just at the walls of ships, but at the desk, clean but for a few framed pictures of his family and one of those lamps on an extendable arm. Next to it, his bed is made neatly with a simple blue comforter. Above the headboard, painted on the wall in old-fashioned-looking script, is a quote that seems vaguely familiar to me: *A ship in the harbor is safe, but that is not what ships are built for.*

My eyes travel down to his nightstand, on which sit a bottle of water, a stack of books, and two rows of orange prescription bottles. I look away from those, knowing he wouldn't want me to see them, back up to the walls of ships. "You collect these?"

Colton clears his throat, nervous or maybe a little embarrassed, I can't tell which. "Sort of. I mean, I made them."

"You *made* them?" There must be hundreds of them, stacked four levels high on all four walls of his room. "*All* of these? Wow."

"Yeah, I don't usually tell people that." He smiles, but his eyes don't meet mine. They're looking over all the bottles too. "It's kind of an old-man hobby."

I can't help but laugh. "It's not an old-man hobby," I say, but it doesn't sound convincing. Probably because it seems like it is.

Colton turns to me now. "No, it really is. My grandpa taught me how to make them a few years back." He pauses, runs his eyes over the walls of ships encased in glass. "He called them 'patience bottles.' Old sailors used to make them out of whatever they could find around their ships when they were stuck out at sea for months at a time. Kind of a way to pass the days."

I watch him look at them, watch the smile slip the tiniest bit from his face, and the things he says start to connect in my mind—"a few years back," "patience bottles."

"I used to have a lot of time on my hands," he fills in, "and I guess he figured it was a good way to pass it. He brought a set over one day and put it down on the desk, and we worked on it together until it was finished." He looks at the one in his hands, and now he smiles again. "You picked up the first one I ever made."

"Can I?" I ask, reaching for the bottle again.

He hands it to me, and I take a closer look at the ship with its tiny sails. "How do you get them inside?"

"Magic," he says.

I bump his shoulder with mine, and the contact sends a little flutter through me. "No, really." I try to sound serious. "How do you do it?"

Colton turns to face me and gently puts his hands over mine on the bottle so that we're holding it together, in the small space between us. He looks at me over the curve of the glass, hands warm on top of mine. "You build the ship outside the bottle so it collapses flat. And then you put it in, and you hope you did everything right, and you pull the string to raise the mast and sails, and if you're lucky, it *is* magic, and they stand up and come to life."

He pauses and looks down through the thick glass at the ship, but I can't take my eyes off him. I can see him sitting here in this room with his grandpa, pale and thin like he was in the pictures, patiently building each tiny ship while he waited for his own form of magic. For the thing that would let *him* stand up and come to life again.

"It's not complicated," he says after a long moment. "Just fragile."

Fragile.

The word catches me, brings me back to what that ER nurse said about Colton's heart. "They're beautiful," I say. "Do you still make them?"

His eyes flicker away for a second, then come back to mine, and he smiles. "Not really. That was . . ." He pauses, seems to catch himself. "No point in building tiny ships that'll never see the ocean when you can be out in the real thing every day."

He smiles, a switch flips, and I can feel that we're done with this conversation. Done here in this room. "Speaking of being out in the ocean," he says, "we should get going so we don't miss the fireworks."

"Okay," I say, not ready to be done here yet. "I just need a minute to change."

Instead of leaving, though, I pause—reach out to him, to his chest. Lightly. Carefully.

Fragile, I think.

But he doesn't feel that way beneath my hand. Not at all. Through all the layers between us—his shirt, the scar that it hides, and the solid curve of his chest— I can almost feel the steady, unmistakable beat of his heart.

My own skips, and a pull, sudden and gravitational, draws me a step closer, into him. We stand there in the doorway like that for a long moment that feels fragile itself. He glances down at my hand on his chest, and though I want to keep it there, to keep feeling this, I let it fall, and I step past him into the hallway, leaving the ships, and that closeness, and the rhythms of both of our heartbeats swirling in the air behind me.

"Light breaks where no sun shines;
Where no sea runs, the waters of the heart
Push in their tides"

—*Dylan Thomas*

CHAPTER TWENTY-TWO

AT FIRST I think the reddish color of the water is a trick of the light. We slip the kayak in just as the sun pulls the last bit of itself below the horizon, leaving behind a deep-orange sky that quickly fades to blue around the edges. The air is still and warm, and the surface of the water is so calm it looks more like a lake than the ocean.

"Wow," I whisper as I help Colton push the kayak into knee-deep water. "It's so pretty out here tonight."

Colton keeps his eyes on the horizon. "I could watch that every day, and it would never get old."

"Me too," I say. *Like this,* I think. Here with my toes digging into the sand, water swirling cool and soft around my legs . . . *with you.*

"Ready?" Colton says, holding the kayak steady for me to get in.

I step in, and he follows a second behind me, and after

we're settled, we dip our paddles into the dark water. We make it easily over one little wave and then another. I look down at my paddle as it pulls through the surface, leaving tiny, rust-colored eddies behind. "Why does the water look like this?" I ask over my shoulder.

"It's a red tide," Colton answers.

"A *red tide*?" I look down again, not liking the sound of it, especially after I let him convince me to paddle from our little cove to the pier in the dark to watch the fireworks from the water. I glance back at him. "I'm scared to ask what that is."

"It's nothing to be scared of," he says. "It's because of a special type of algae that blooms all of a sudden, all up and down the coast. It's pretty amazing when it happens."

"Really?" I keep my eyes on the water as we glide slowly over it. It looks more dirty than amazing.

"Yeah. It's just this random thing—nobody can really predict or control it, I guess because nobody really even knows what causes it, but at night . . ."

He trails off, and when I turn around, his face is all lit up in a way that's become familiar to me. It makes me smile. "At night, what?" I ask.

He looks out over the water like he's debating whether or not he should answer, then shoots me a dimpled grin. "Just wait. You'll see."

"Now I'm *really* scared to ask."

Colton laughs. "It's nothing to be scared of, promise." He points with his paddle at the silhouette of the pier in the distance. "C'mon. We're gonna have to move faster than this if we wanna make it down there in time for the fireworks to start."

I look at the pier jutting out into the ocean against a quickly dimming sky. "It looks kind of far. . . . Are you sure we'll make it back? We won't get lost at sea? Or eaten by the nighttime red tide or anything?"

"I can't make any promises," Colton says with a shrug. "Those are all risks I'm willing to take tonight." He smiles, calm and confident, completely at home on the water and in the moment, and I can feel that buzz in the air between us again.

"Risks you're willing to take, huh?"

He nods slowly and tries to look serious. "For your benefit, of course."

"Well then," I say, unable to keep a smile from my face. "In that case, I guess I'm willing too."

"Good," Colton says, and I'm pretty sure that this time it's the answer he was both hoping for *and* expecting. He doesn't take his eyes from mine as the smile sneaks back over his face. "You won't regret it."

The sky goes indigo and the first stars emerge, tiny and bright above the ocean as we move smoothly over its surface. My strokes are strong, so full of nervous energy at first that I'm sure I could paddle to the horizon and back without feeling a thing. But after few quiet moments, we slip into our familiar, wordless rhythm, and I relax and find my way back into that place that makes everything disappear except for the ocean, and the sky, and us—gliding together through that invisible place where one ends and the other begins.

My eyes adjust by degrees to the darkness, at almost the same rate it falls around us. I close them for a moment to let the air and water and night sink in. Everything feels electric. Vibrant, and alive, and charged with possibility. Sailing over the water, through the dark, I do too. It's a feeling that starts deep in my chest and spreads out, wide and expansive. Almost too much to contain. I flash to the picture on my dresser, the red glass heart encased safely in its bottle, and then to all of Colton's ships in theirs, and that's when I realize the truth in the words scrawled over the wall above them: *A ship in the harbor is safe, but that is not what ships are meant for.*

This is what they're meant for, this feeling right here. And maybe . . . maybe it's what hearts are meant for too.

My eyes are still closed when I feel Colton's rhythm skip a stroke, and I know he's lifted his paddle from the water. "There it is," he says from behind me, his voice full of excitement. "Quinn—do you see it?"

I open my eyes, and he leans forward as far as he can,

drawing his paddle through the water next to me. For a second I'm sure my eyes are playing tricks on me. Night has fallen completely, the lights of the pier shine in the distance, and the stars dot the sky above us; but in the place where his paddle cuts through the surface of the water, a pale-blue glow emerges. I blink, and it's gone.

"Did you see it?" Colton asks, and before I can answer, he draws his paddle through the water again. Again, a faint-blue glow appears and disappears just as quickly as it came.

"What *is* that?" I ask. I watch the water, waiting for it to happen again.

"It's the water," Colton says. He laughs softly as he dips one end of his paddle in, swirling it around hard and igniting another blue glow, brighter this time than the last.

"But . . ." I don't finish. Instead I do the same with my own paddle and am amazed when the same glow appears around it. I laugh out loud. There's no logical explanation for this . . . this . . . I don't even know what to call it.

I can feel Colton watching me. "I was hoping we'd be able to see it," he says.

"What is *it*?" I'm still swirling my paddle around in disbelief.

"It's called bioluminescence," he says. "It's all that algae I was telling you about." He uses his paddle to scoop up some of the water and lets it roll off the end, and when the drops hit the surface, they create a tiny, barely discernible blue light. I can't make out Colton's features now, dark as it is, but I can tell from his voice he's grinning from ear to ear.

"How do they . . ." I sweep my paddle through the water again, still trying to understand how something like this can be real.

"It's their defense mechanism," he says. "Like a reflex. When something touches them, they respond with light." He sweeps his paddle out in a wide arc, and the soft-blue glow appears again, somehow more special now because of why it happens. Because when these tiny little things are afraid, they shine.

"This is . . . it's magical." I swirl my paddle around gently again. I am giddy—with the night, and the water, and the glow. And with Colton for showing them all to me. For giving them to me, really.

"How do you know so much about so much?" I ask.

Colton laughs. "Is that a trick question?"

"No, I mean . . ."

I bite my lip, wish I could take back the question, because what I mean scares me. What I *mean* is how does he somehow know to show me things I didn't realize I needed to see, or take me places I wouldn't have guessed I needed to go? When Trent died, it was like I took a step back from life altogether because I saw how fragile it really is. But Colton—he's been pulling me back in since the moment we met. Showing me the beautiful side of the very same truth.

"Never mind," I say after a moment. "I don't know what I mean."

A low boom echoes in the distance, and I'm thankful when it draws Colton's attention away from me.

"First one of the night," he says, lifting his chin toward the sky. I turn in time to see a trail of white streak up the sky, then explode into brilliant, glimmering bits of light that arch down over the water like a giant chandelier. Colton takes his paddle from his lap. "Let's go."

"I don't even need fireworks with this in the water," I say, still swirling my own paddle. The effect of the soft-blue light has not worn off on me.

"It's the Fourth of July; everyone needs fireworks," Colton says. "C'mon." He digs his paddle in and gets us moving, and I join him, only now I keep my eyes wide-open, soak in as much as I possibly can as we head for the pier, cutting a soft, glowing blue path through the night and its darkness.

We paddle toward the deep booms and exploding lights, and after a few minutes we're close enough that I can smell the sulfury smoke and feel each firework deep in my chest. People all over the beach cheer as a red, white, and blue one lights up the night above them, then crackles down all around. We paddle even closer to the pier, and in the bursts of color and light from above I can see the water surging gently against the mussel-covered pilings. Colton lifts his paddle from the water and stows it inside the kayak, so I do the same and then turn around.

"Okay," he says. "You wanna see them from the best seat in the house?"

"Isn't that where we are right now?" I ask, without taking my eyes from the sky.

"Almost. Hang on."

Another boom echoes in my chest, and I shiver in the suddenly cool air. The kayak rocks, and Colton tosses something that lands in the water with a heavy plunk and a splash.

"Anchor," he says. "So we don't drift."

I nod as he leans forward into the dip of my seat and unclips the seat pad. I can't see much of anything, but his hands know their way around.

"Put this down where your feet were, like a pillow. I'll keep us balanced."

I lift myself up enough to pull the pad from beneath me and manage to get it to the foot well, then Colton hands me three folded towels. "Here," he says. "Use these for padding. Then you can lie back and put your legs up over the middle right here." He pats the flat divide that separates our two seats.

"What about you?"

"I'll do the same thing in a sec."

"Okay."

For a moment we fumble around, each of us moving slightly to try to accommodate the other, unsure of where to put our limbs in such close proximity to each other. I get the towels smoothed over the pad as best I can, then carefully lower myself down onto it like he said.

Once I'm sitting, it only takes Colton a second to make the switch with his seat, and he lowers himself into it slowly, stretching his legs out next to mine on the raised section between us. The kayak bobs gently as we lie there settling in, the lengths of our legs brushed right up against each other. Heat courses up mine, despite the coolness of the night air.

"*Now* we have the best seats in the house," Colton says. Red light explodes above us, making him look as flushed as I feel.

It takes an effort to pull my eyes from him, but I lie back all the way and look up. The next firework shoots high, a vertical white streak in the sky above us, and after the tiniest delay when I wonder if maybe it won't ignite, brilliant blue light explodes above us, then falls, soft and slow, before it vanishes into the air around us.

We lie there watching the fireworks explode and fall around us, and I can feel the boom-crackle of them in my chest, and the heat of his legs tangled up with mine, and with each moment that ticks by, something else grows stronger. A thing I couldn't have predicted, and now something I can't control or explain. It's a pull I don't want to fight anymore—I *can't* fight anymore.

The boat rocks gently as I sit up, and I'm not surprised when Colton is there already. I know he feels it too. We sit there, wordless, face-to-face in the glow above and below us. So much light after so much dark.

He raises a hand to my cheek, weaving his fingers back into my hair, and then he runs his thumb, feather-soft, over the tiny scar on my bottom lip.

That moment I first saw him and our worlds collided comes rushing back. Sends shivers all through me. I lean into the warmth of his touch, exhale a shaky breath as I bring my fingertips to his chest.

"Quinn, I . . ." He whispers the words, unfinished, into my mouth as the space between us disappears and our lips finally touch. A thousand fireworks explode inside me, and I feel them in him too, in his lips on mine, and his hands in my hair, and the way we pull each other closer.

Everything else falls away, and in this moment, when we touch, we are light.

"One of the hardest things in life is having words in your heart that you can't utter."

—James Earl Jones

CHAPTER TWENTY-THREE

AS WE PADDLE back in the darkness, the only thing I can see in front of me is the line I've crossed—and it's blinding. I can still feel Colton's lips on mine, and the want in his touch, strong and gentle at the same time. And I can hear the sound of my name, whispered on his lips. But the thing I *see* when I close my eyes is his face, in that moment just before that kiss. Open. Trusting. Unaware of the truths I've danced around, truths that feel like they've grown into lies now because I've left them unspoken for this long.

We paddle in a silence that feels more tense than comfortable to me, and I wonder as we make our way over the water if Colton senses it too. When we reach the shore, I'm positive he must. He doesn't say anything but shoots me a quick smile as we lift the kayak together and carry it, dripping and cold, over our heads to his bus. After we load it up, he reaches into his backpack and hands me a dry towel. "Here you go," he says. "I'll be— I'll let you change."

"Thank you," I say, and he disappears around to the driver's side to give me space.

As I stand there alone, the air feels colder than it did out on the water. Even with the towel wrapped tightly around me, I shiver as I peel off my bathing suit beneath it and fumble with shaking hands for my dress. Through the windows, I can see Colton's outline as he pulls his rash guard up over his head and reaches in, to his seat, for his shirt. I look down, try to focus on making my fingers button Ryan's dress, but Colton's door opens and I catch a glimpse of him in the dome light, hair messy from the salty breeze, cheeks flushed with the cool of the night, lips that tasted of both when he kissed me. A light, fluttery feeling rises in my chest, sends a rush of warmth all through me as his door closes and the cab goes dark again. I take a deep breath, then exhale long and slow. I don't have any other choice but to tell him—especially when I feel like I do right now.

I finish dressing slowly, deliberately. Wrap and rewrap my wet bathing suit in the towel. Take another deep breath, close my eyes, and replay that kiss one more time before I reach for the handle on the passenger door. When I open it, Colton gives me one look, then turns the key and reaches for the heater knob on the dash. "I'm sorry—I should've gotten the heater going. You look cold."

I nod as I get in, cupping my hands to my mouth like the cold is to blame rather than what I'm about to say. Then I shut the door and swallow hard. *Just say it. Tell him.*

"Colton, there's something—"

"You wanna go spa-hopping?"

We speak at the same time, our words overlapping, intercepting each other.

He laughs. "Sorry. You first."

"I . . ." I hesitate, and the little nerve I've worked up drains right out of me when a smile tugs at the corners of his mouth. "Go *what*?" I ask.

"Spa-hopping," he says, eyes shining in the glow from the dash. "The Sandcastle Inn has a good one on the roof, and I know the code. We could get in for a little while. Warm up."

He sounds so hopeful that I let myself picture, for a second, sitting in a rooftop spa with him, steam rising up into the night air, hot water swirling around us, and—

"I can't," I say too quickly. "I—I need to go home." I reach over my shoulder for my seat belt and click it in like a final decision.

"I don't understand," Colton says. The smile is gone from his voice.

His eyes search for some reason for the way I've gone from so close to so faraway, drifting in the dark. I look down at my hands in my lap, and I don't say anything. I *can't* say anything.

An alarm beeps from his phone on the dash, and he

reaches out and silences it without even looking at it.

I glance at the phone. Wish he wouldn't ignore it, because I know it's a med reminder.

Colton clears his throat, straightens up in his seat. "Back there on the water, that was . . ."

My eyes drift back to him, every bit of me wanting to hear the rest of that sentence. Wanting to know what he thought it was. But he just looks down and drums his fingers on the steering wheel, watching them for a long moment. "I'm sorry," he says. "I thought you felt . . ." He shakes his head, puts the bus in drive. "Never mind. I'll take you back to your car."

He turns the wheel, and we roll forward slowly, onto the road to his house, and to him not knowing the truth—not about Trent, or his heart, or what I felt out there too.

"Stop," I say softly. Colton presses the brake down and looks over at me, and I see hope without caution. "I did," I say. "Feel that way."

Relief floods his face, and I try to be as brave and honest as he was just a moment ago.

"Out on the water was . . ." I pause, gathering my courage. "Was the first time I've felt like that in a long time. Since . . ." It's so close, the truth, rising to the surface again. "Since I lost someone really close to me," I say, finding my voice. "Someone I loved." There's a small measure of relief in the tiny bit of truth, but it's short-lived.

"I know," Colton says, looking down at the steering wheel.

Everything in me—breath, pulse, thought—stops.

"You *know*?"

His eyes run over me, and I don't see any of the things I'm waiting for—hurt, anger—none of it. The only thing I can feel from him in this moment is sympathy. "I thought," he says quietly. "You hold back—the way people sometimes do when they've lost someone." He pauses. "Or when they think they're going to. I had a girlfriend a couple of years ago who got like that when things—" He clears his throat. "She held back with me that way. The way you do."

My heart leaps back into action, alternately pounding out guilt and worry and relief against my ribs. He doesn't know he's talking about Trent, but he can see more than I realize.

"I'm so sorry," I say. "I should've told you sooner, but I've been . . ."

Holding back for more reasons than just feeling guilty about Trent. Holding back because I'm afraid of what will happen if you know the truth. What I'll lose.

A lump rises in the back of my throat, and tears well up, ready to overflow with what I know I need to say next.

"Don't be sorry," Colton says, leaning closer. He brings his lips, so softly, to my forehead in a kiss that asks nothing in return. I close my eyes and let the feeling of it sink in, and wish it were that simple.

His lips move to my temple, trail down my cheek, and linger there, a breath away from mine. "You told me that," he whispers, "not to be sorry for the things you have no control over."

Our lips brush, and I feel like there isn't anything I want to hold back. I almost sink into him, into another kiss, but he pulls away, just enough so we're eye to eye in the darkness between us.

"Please," he whispers, "don't be sorry for anything. Especially this."

"Nothing is less in our power than the heart, and far from commanding we are forced to obey it."

—Jean-Jacques Rousseau

CHAPTER TWENTY-FOUR

I DRIVE HOME in silence. Dark, heavy silence, broken only by an occasional set of passing headlights. I see flashes of tonight: the sunset, the glow of the water, the fireworks, that kiss. And flashes of another night and another kiss.

The first time Trent kissed me, we were night swimming in my pool. Late, after everyone else was asleep. I'd swum past him under the water, feeling my hair ripple behind me in the light and hoping my silhouette looked as pretty as I felt right then. When I came up, he was there in front of me. His hands just barely grazed my waist, and we balanced there on that moment, wondering and knowing at the same time what was about to happen. Our first kiss was soft, sweet. A question on my lips. He tasted like the watermelon bubble gum he was always chewing, and the stolen summer night. The memory produces a tiny ache around my heart, a kind of longing that feels distant and nostalgic.

The feel of his lips on mine is just a whisper of a memory.

But the memory of Colton's is vivid and alive. Where Trent's first kiss was shy, timid, a question, kissing Colton was like already knowing the answer. Knowing that answer was each other.

But there is so much tangled up in us, and all around us. Loss and guilt. Secrets and lies. So many things he doesn't know, things that I *am* sorry for because I *do* have control over them. Or I thought I did until tonight. I thought I did until I recognized that long-forgotten falling sensation I didn't know I would feel again. Didn't know I *could* feel again.

When I pull into the driveway, the house is dark, and I sit for a moment and look out the window at the sky so full of stars it looks like it can't really exist. Like something so beautiful and so fragile couldn't really be true. And then the light in Ryan's room switches on, and all I want is for her to tell me it can.

She jumps a little when I burst through her bedroom door without knocking. "Hey, how was your—" Her smile falls at the sight of me. "What's wrong?"

That's all it takes. I make it the few steps to the bed where she's sitting before I crumple into her, and everything I've been holding back unravels.

"Hey, hey, hey," she says, putting her arms around me. "What's going on, what happened?"

I close my eyes tight and curl into myself as my shoulders shake in her arms.

"Quinn," she says, pulling me away from her enough to look at me. "What happened?"

I see it again, our kiss. "I . . . he . . ." Then I hear his words, *Please don't be sorry for anything. Especially this*, and I bite my bottom lip, run my hands over my face that's hot and wet with tears.

"He *what*." She sits up straight now, concern etching itself deeper into her expression.

I shake my head. "We kissed, out on the water, and it was so . . . and I . . ." My voice hitches, and another sob drops my chin to my chest.

Ryan's voice goes gentle again. "We talked about this already, about how it's okay to feel—"

"It's not," I say, looking up to meet her eyes.

"Quinn, it *is*. You have to believe me on this. You and Trent—"

"It's not *that*!"

The edge in my voice surprises us both, and she's silent as she looks at me, taking in my puffy eyes and trembling chin.

"Then . . . what is it?" she asks slowly. Like she's afraid to know the answer.

I swallow over the tears that are thick in my throat, and over my own fear of what she'll think. "I did something awful," I whisper. I look down, away from my sister's eyes, at my hands twisting in my lap. "Something I should never have done, and now . . ."

My palm comes to my mouth to hold back the rising sob, and the words I know I need to say out loud.

I can feel my sister's eyes on me, but I don't meet them. "What? Just tell me. Whatever it is."

I hesitate for a tiny moment, and then I do what she says.

I tell her everything, beginning with the letter I wrote. I tell her about the days I waited for an answer, and the nights I searched for him. I tell her about Shelby's blog, and how I finally found him. About how I never meant to meet him, but once I did, I wanted to know him. And how now that I know him, the last thing I want to do is hurt him. And then I tell her about our kiss tonight. The way it felt, and what he said after, about holding back and being sorry. And finally, when I've told her everything and there are no words left for what I've done, I look at my sister.

She is quiet for a very long time after I finish. I sit on her bed, surrounded by tissues, puffy eyed and waiting for her to tell me that it's going to be okay, or that he'll understand, or that it's not as bad as it seems, but she doesn't. She takes a deep breath. Looks at me like she's sorry for what she's about to say.

"You have to tell him."

"I know," I say, and the acknowledgment sets off a fresh

wave of tears in me, but Ryan doesn't hold back.

"Not just because he deserves to know the truth," she says. "You need to tell him because it's the only chance you have for anything between the two of you to be real, if that's what you want."

She looks at me now, eyes serious. "But first you have to actually decide what you want. You're halfway there, I think, but . . ."

She pauses, presses her lips together, and then says something else I already know, deep down in a place that's hidden away.

"If you want to open yourself up to Colton, you have to let go of Trent first. Let him be a part of who you are— your first love, your memories, your past. But let him go. You have to," she says softly, "so that you can be here now."

"And you would accept the seasons of your heart just as you have always accepted that seasons pass over your fields.

"And you would watch with serenity through the winter of your grief."

—*Kahlil Gibran*

CHAPTER TWENTY-FIVE

I FINISH TYING my shoelaces and stand up. Look at my reflection in the mirror. Breathe. And then I let my eyes wander over the pictures of me and Trent. I follow them, all along the edge of the mirror, to the sunflower he gave me, hanging pale and dry next to them. I take one more deep breath, and then I reach out and cradle it in my hands, as gently as I can.

I glance down at the picture I cut out from Ryan's magazine. The heart, washed up on the shore of an empty beach, encased in glass. I look at it and think about what Colton said about all his ships in their bottles—how he didn't want to build them anymore if they were never going to see the ocean—and I understand.

I feel the same way.

I slip out the front door as quietly as I can, because I need to do this alone. My legs carry me down the steps and over the dirt, and I start to breathe again. My heart starts to work again.

I feel my feet hit the ground, one in front of the other, until I get to the end of the driveway. And then I stop. Breathe. And I begin again, down the road I've been avoiding for so long. The road that was the beginning of us, to the place I thought was the end of me.

It's been so long since I've run this way that it looks unfamiliar at first. The trees are fuller, the grape vines thicker. But I know this road. I know its rolling hills, and I know its turns. I know the stretch where the sunflowers grew wild in the field and along the fence.

Where they still do.

They're brilliant against the summer sky, swaying gently in the breeze. I stop to listen, and I can almost hear his voice.

"Hey! Wait!"

I close my eyes, and I can see him there, smiling, holding a sunflower in his hand. But then another memory pushes its way in. The splintered fence, swirling lights, petals and blood spread over the ground.

I open my eyes and I'm back here, now, where the ground shows no scars, and the fence has been mended, and the sunflowers grow tall and beautiful all around it.

I fix my eyes on the field of gold as I take the dried flower I am holding and raise my hand above my head. I watch the tall stalks bend and sway when I roll the papery petals between my fingers and release each tiny piece into the breeze. All our firsts, and our lasts, and everything in between. They swirl and dance on the invisible currents, and then one by one, they disappear to a place they will always be a part of.

"Fear can paralyze people. One reason recipients don't write is because they are afraid they will hurt or harm the family somehow by 'bringing up something they don't want to think about,' the loss of their loved one. Of course, what they don't realize is that this is a loss that you carry every day. . . . Another deterrent to writing is the time it takes for the recipient to heal physically and psychologically from the transplant. A recipient has to take a myriad of drugs to avoid any possibility of rejection. This procedure of balancing the amounts needed of the drugs can take months or longer. The trauma to the body and spirit is immense."

—Karen Hannahs, Intermountain Donor Services: "Why Don't They Write?"

CHAPTER TWENTY-SIX

FEAR IS A hard, heavy knot in my stomach when I pull up to the kayak shop. I have to force myself out of the car. The door to the shop is propped open with a scuba tank, and the sign says OPEN, but when I poke my head through the doorway, I don't see anyone behind the counter. I hover there, neither in nor out, my sister's words running through my mind.

You have to tell him. He deserves to know.

I knew these things before she told me—it was the fear of losing him that kept me quiet. But standing here now, I realize what I fear even more is hurting him. I picture his face when I say the words, and my resolve to tell him starts to drain out of me. It takes all my strength to hold on to it. After a long moment I take a deep breath and cross the threshold into the shop. Its racks of equipment are clean and bright in the early-afternoon light, and a fan oscillates slowly, blowing the now-familiar smell of plastic and neoprene my way. I glance around, half expecting Colton to come from the back room carrying a full scuba tank or a set of life jackets and wearing a wide grin, but he doesn't. Nobody does.

I take a few tentative steps toward the back room, and that's when I hear a voice, just above the low whir of the fan.

"Would you *stop* already?" I barely recognize it as Colton's, the way it cuts through the words. "It was a mistake," he says, "and you need to let it go."

I go still right where I'm standing.

"Please don't get mad at me, Colton." The other voice is Shelby's, and there's an edge to hers too. "I just want to make sure you realize you can't *make* that mistake. You don't get to. The second you start missing your meds, you risk going into rejection—don't you get that? You could *die*."

I don't dare move. I try not to breathe.

Shelby goes on. "So you never get to make that mistake, Colton—not because you're tired, or they make you feel crappy, or you're . . . distracted." She sighs.

The knot in my gut twists itself tighter.

"Distracted?" Colton spits the word back at her. "By what? A girl? *Living?* It's been over a year. Am I still supposed to sit around and take my vitals and watch the clock for my next dose, and think about the fact that it's all on borrowed time? Should I focus on that?"

Shelby's voice turns angry. "Do you realize how selfish you sound right now? How ungrateful?"

No, no, no.

If her words knock the air right out of me, I can't imagine what they've just done to Colton. The silence that follows is excruciatingly long, and it takes everything in me now not to creep closer and step in between them.

"Wow," he says finally. His voice is flat. Cold. "You really just went there." He clears his throat. Laughs, but it's joyless. Angry. "I'm done."

There are footsteps. The quick shuffle of his flip-flops over the floor, heading toward the doorway. My fear unravels into panic at being discovered, and I look around for a place to hide—not just from Colton and Shelby, but from all the things I came to tell him.

"Really? You're done?" Shelby shoots back, and the footsteps stop. "What about that letter? It's been over a year for that too, Colton." Her voice has gone all calm again, but it's false, the kind you put on when you know you've fired an arrow that'll win you the fight.

She has no idea how far that arrow reaches.

The rising panic in my chest turns into something heavy and thick that spreads out all at once, my heart pumping it into every last cell of me, like blood. It sits there, rooting my feet to the cement floor as the room begins to spin.

I sink down against the wall behind me. *That letter.*

"I'm sorry," Shelby says. Her voice is softer now, regret creeping in at its edges, but she goes on. "I get that it's hard. And I know you'll write his parents when you're ready. But you should at least answer the letter *you* got. That poor girl lost her boyfriend, and tried to reach out to you, and you can't just leave something like that unanswered. Do you know what that must feel like?"

That poor girl.

There is no air in the room. Not where I sit, eyes squeezed shut against tears that want to spill down my cheeks. *That poor girl who tried to reach out to you. Who found you when you didn't answer. Who's been lying to you since the day you met.*

It's silent for what feels like an eternity, and the tension stretches so tight between the walls of the shop, I know it's going to snap any second.

Shelby pushes on, even as I beg in my mind for her to stop. "Maybe it'll make you feel better, to answer it," she says. "Maybe it'll remind you that it's a gift, Colton. Not a burden."

I feel Colton snap before he even speaks.

"Do you think I *need* a reminder?" His voice is all sharp edges and open wounds. "You don't think the med schedule, or the cardio therapy, or the biopsies are enough? Or the scar on my chest? You don't think that's enough?"

"Colton, I—"

"Not a day goes by that I'm not reminded, over and over. How *lucky* I am. That I should be grateful. That I should be happy just to *be* here." He pauses, clears his throat. "That the only reason I am is because that guy—someone's boyfriend, son, brother, friend—died."

His words, and the way he says "that guy," like Trent is a total stranger, knock the air out of me though I'm already down, crouched on my heels against the wall. A flicker of anger lights up somewhere in me now too—at him, and at myself. Out of all the rules I broke to find Colton, withholding Trent's name in the letter was the one I actually followed. Now I wish I hadn't. I wish I'd written it all down, every detail of who Trent was, so he'd know who "that guy" was. Maybe then he would've written back.

My hands are shaking, and now a part of me wants to step out from the shadows. Ask him the questions I somehow forgot I wanted the answers to.

The air is thick with silent tension, then Colton goes on. "Do you know what *that* feels like, Shelby? How am I supposed to answer a letter like that? Tell her I'm so sorry about her boyfriend? Promise her I'll take care of his heart? That I'll think about it every day and never forget that I'm here because he's not?"

Colton's voice catches. "Don't you get it? That's what I want. I want to forget, all of it. Why is that so horrible? To want a normal life?"

"Colton, that's not what I—" There's a small shuffle, like maybe she took a step toward him.

"Leave it alone," he says. "Leave *me* alone." He pauses, and in the quiet, my own heart thunders in my ears. "I don't need any more reminders."

I push myself up onto my feet. Concentrate on putting one foot in front of the other, swift, desperate, silent. I need to get away.

I almost make it to the door before I feel the warm, familiar weight of his hand on my shoulder.

"*Quinn?*" Colton says. "What're you—" The edge is still there in his voice, though I can tell he's trying to hide it for my sake.

I bite the inside of my cheek. I know I should turn

around and meet his eyes, for his sake. But I don't. I can't.

"Hey," he says gently, turning me so we're face-to-face.

We lock eyes, and I can see the storm in his, their usual bright green clouded over by the furrow of his brows. He looks like he wants to escape just as much as I do.

I glance over his shoulder toward the back room, willing Shelby not to come out and see me here. "I'm sorry, I should've called first, I—"

Colton's eyes flick back in the direction of his sister and everything he doesn't want to be reminded of, and I feel a stab of guilt when they come back to me with no idea that it's all right here. Right in front of him.

"No, I'm glad you're here. It's just . . ." His hand comes to my shoulder, and I try to ignore the complicated rush his touch sends through me. Try not to look him in the eye.

"Wait," he says. "Come with me."

"Where?" I ask without meaning to. Looking at him without meaning to.

"Anywhere," he says. "It doesn't matter. Please, just . . . come with me."

The need in his voice washes over me like a wave, finding its way in through the tiniest cracks, into the deepest, farthest places. It makes me want to wrap my arms around him, and it makes me want to run away; but I don't do either one of those things.

I've never seen him hurt like this. Lost. I look at him

standing there in front of me, and I can feel, in that moment, how much he needs me.

How much I need him too.

I search for any sign that he knows the truth about the girl who wrote that letter, but there's none.

Without saying a word, I nod, and he takes my hand, and we go. Anywhere but here.

"We can only be said to be alive in those moments when our hearts are conscious of our treasures."

—*Thornton Wilder*

CHAPTER TWENTY-SEVEN

WE DRIVE. WINDOWS open, wind swirling wild around us, filling the space of our silence with cool salt air. I can feel the tension rolling off Colton as he shifts and turns. I don't know where we're going, but it doesn't matter. We drive like that, trying to block out the noise of our thoughts with the sound of the wind; and it's not until we're out of town, on the empty two-lane coast highway, heading north into the rolling hills, that Colton's shoulders, and his grip on the steering wheel, relax the slightest bit.

"You ever been up to Big Sur?" he asks, his voice heavier than normal. It's clear in this question that he doesn't plan on acknowledging the fight he just had with Shelby in the store, but I can't let it go, not anymore.

"Colton . . . ," I say tentatively.

He glances at me out of the corner of his eye. "There's this place up there called McWay Falls. It's probably my favorite place, but I haven't been there in a long time. It has the clearest, bluest water you've ever seen. Some days you can see twenty feet, straight to the bottom. And there's a waterfall that comes down off the cliff, right onto the sand. I've been wanting to take you there," he adds with a smile. That familiar optimism has crept back into his voice, and he sounds more like himself now. Or more like the Colton he lets me see. "We could grab some food on the way, eat at the falls, take the kayak out, have a perfect day—"

"Colton." My voice comes out firmer this time, and I hope it's enough to say to him that we can't ignore what just happened. That as much as we both may want to, we can't go any further with so much left unspoken between us.

He sighs. Looks out his side window for a brief moment before bringing his eyes back to the road. "I just want to get outta here for a little while." He shifts in his seat, thrums his fingers on the steering wheel. "That, back there with my sister . . ."

"It's okay," I say quickly. I can see how uncomfortable he is, and it weakens my resolve to talk about it. "You don't have to explain. Mine can be the same way when she gets worried, and it's between you guys anyway, and . . ."

Now I'm talking around it. Again.

"So you heard that whole thing," Colton says.

I look out my window, out to the hills covered in rolling summer-gold grasses, away from the words I keep replaying over and over. Shelby's words, and his. And then I tell him the truth.

"I did. But it's not any of my business, I—"

"It's okay," Colton says. "I wasn't trying to keep it secret from you." He glances over at me. "Not really." The word *secret* sticks in my gut, and though I feel his gaze linger on me, I can't meet it. I roll down the window even farther, wishing the wind would just swirl in and carry all our secrets away.

"Anyway," he says, shifting in his seat again, "there's not a whole lot to tell." He slides his eyes back to the road. "I got really sick a few years back—a viral infection that got into my heart and tore it up so bad I needed a new one. I got put on the transplant list, spent a lot of time waiting, in and out of the hospital, until last year when I finally got a new heart."

I inhale sharply. I know all this already, but to hear him tell it himself hits me in a whole different way.

Colton pauses, and in the edge of that pause I can hear all the things he doesn't say to me. The things he said to Shelby about Trent, and the letter. The things about how his life was during that time, and how it is now. I wait, quiet. Brace myself for him to say them to me, but he doesn't. He just keeps his eyes on the sharp curve of the road and gives the slightest nod, like that's it, that's all there is.

I nod slowly in answer, like I'm hearing all this for the first time, like it's all that simple, but it takes everything in me to keep my breaths even, my face neutral. The way he put it, like that's the whole story, feels like a closed door meant to keep me out. Maybe it's to keep me safe from it all, but it's far too late. I know too much for that.

I know that behind all the pictures of him smiling through it and beneath the surface of Shelby's posts about how positive her brother was through it all, I know there was pain, and suffering, and guilt. There was sickness, and weakness, and being hospitalized. Losing weight, and swelling up, and procedure after procedure. Machines, and tubes, and endless medications. Soaring hopes, and crashing letdowns. Fund-raisers, and family vigils. Big scares and little victories.

There was life lived from behind the glass of the hospital and the confines of his house while his friends and family felt the ocean air in their lungs, and sunlight and water on their skin. There was a roomful of ships that would never leave their clear-glass ports. But he smiled for the camera every time. And he traded death for more than just a lifetime of medical care. He traded it for an anchor of guilt.

I can't handle the thought of making it any worse. Not now. Not when I know how much all that still hurts him. I turn my face to the window so that the air rushing in will be a good excuse for the tears that prick hot at my eyes.

"It's okay," Colton says. "I'm good now." He smiles, trying to lighten the tone, and brings a fist to his chest. "Strong. And it was gonna come out sooner or later." He shrugs. "I guess I just really liked that you knew me without all that."

"Why?" I ask, my voice barely above a whisper.

He tilts his head, considering, then opens his mouth to say something but reels it back in. I look straight ahead, try to give him space to find his answer as we round another sharp curve. The road hugs the mountain high above the ocean, and from the passenger side I can't see the drop, which I'm thankful for.

What I can see is the sky, and the ocean spreading out from the cliffs, wide and sparkling in the afternoon sun. It makes me wish we were out there in the kayak, floating on one of the aquamarine, sun-soaked patches of water, in that safe place between the ocean and the sky, where nothing else matters but the moment.

Colton shrugs. "Because I don't think about any of that when I'm with you, and that's—" He stops. Smiles, but not like the smile I know. There's a vulnerability in this one, and in his eyes. "That was a pretty dark time of my life, and you . . ."

He glances over at me again, eyes serious. "You're like light, after all that."

I come undone right there. Tears wells up, and I take his

hand in mine and hold on, and try to hold them back, as I see it all. Me, noticing him for the first time in the café, him standing on my doorstep with the sunflower in his hand, the two of us inside the hollowed-out rock with the sunlight streaming in and then paddling over the surface of the water, silhouetted between a glowing ocean and a sky exploding with fireworks.

I can't risk losing it all. All of this light.

He's looking at me, waiting for me to say something back, to say I feel the same way. The road in front of us pins itself into a curve so sharp, it forces Colton's eyes back to the road, forces him to slow down, and like so many other moments, forces me into him, and this time I don't fight it.

Leaned into him, I catch a glimpse of the cliff's edge, and the ocean and the wave-crashed rocks far, far below, and for a brief moment it feels like my toes are hanging over the edge and I'm deciding whether or not to jump. But then I realize I already have. I've fallen so far, so fast that I didn't see it happening, and now there's no going back, nothing to hold on to but him.

"Occasionally in life there are those moments of unutterable fulfillment which cannot be completely explained by those symbols called words. Their meanings can only be articulated by the inaudible language of the heart."

—Martin Luther King Jr.

CHAPTER TWENTY-EIGHT

AFTER MILES OF twisting turns, sheer cliff on one side and lush green hillside with ravines and tiny waterfalls on the other, the highway finally winds inland just a bit, and we pass a small sign that reads STATE CAMPGROUND. Colton doesn't turn into the campground but makes a left into a parking lot on the coastal side of the highway. There's no one in the kiosk to take our money, and since the parking lot is deserted, we have our pick of spots. Colton pulls the bus up next to the fence, under a cypress tree that spreads its rich green branches out wide and flat, like an enormous bonsai tree.

It's quiet when he looks over. "I can't believe you're here with me." He leans across the seat and gives me a kiss, and I can feel a smile on his lips. "This is my favorite place. Ever. Come on."

We both get out and stand near our open doors, stretching in the afternoon sun. The air is different here: cooler, and more layered. The smell of the salt water mixes with scents of the trees and flowers that grow wild and tumble over the hill. We can't see or hear the ocean from where we stand, but I can feel it, just like I can feel the last bit of tension slip off Colton as he breathes it in too.

"Let's go see the water," he says, and before I can answer, he grabs my hand and leads me to a short wooden staircase that goes up and over the fence, to the other side, where a trail winds through the tall green grass, then disappears at the edge of the bluff. We climb up and over, then walk, hand in hand, down the trail. We don't say anything, but we don't have to. The sweetness of the air, and the feel of each other's hand, the distant sound of the ocean—all of it is perfect. All of it feels like what we need, and where we should be.

When we get to where the trail leads to a steep set of stairs, the view of the ocean unfolds in front of us. It stops me in my tracks.

"Wow," I breathe. "This is beautiful."

"I knew you'd love it," Colton says with a grin as he runs his eyes over the wide cove of sapphire water below. At the southern end of it, a graceful white arc of water dives over the cliff and spills out onto the sand before meeting the ocean. Colton inhales deep and slow, like he's drinking it all in, comparing every little detail to the picture in his memory.

"How long has it been since you've been here?" I ask.

He doesn't take his eyes from the water. "A long time. It was with my dad, maybe ten years ago? We came camping, just us, right on the beach." He smiles. "Brought the kayak and our surfboards and stayed in the water all day, then came in and cooked hot dogs and s'mores over the campfire, and watched the shooting stars over the ocean at night."

"Sounds perfect."

"It was. A perfect day. I remember it that way anyway. Thought about it a lot when I was sick." He glances at me. "I thought maybe that would go down as my best day."

We both watch as a wave, much bigger than what I've seen in Shelter Cove, rises, gathering speed and height, then crashes in a fast line with a thunder I can hear, even this far away.

Colton lets out a low whistle. "You feeling brave?"

"Not that brave," I say as the next wave does a repeat, shooting white water high up into the air when it crashes. "It's wilder up here."

He nods. "Yeah, it's not really kayak friendly out there." We watch as another wave peels across the cove in a perfect, empty line. "Good surf, though."

I watch it, amused by the fact that every time I've heard him say that, my thought is that it looks downright scary. I still like catching the white water next to the pier.

"You can surf if you want, I don't mind. I'll watch." The platform we're standing on has a bench and a view, and I know it would do him some good to get in the water.

"Really? You wouldn't mind?"

"No, go. I'm not quite ready for those waves yet, but I've seen what you can do. "

He turns to me and smiles, then pulls me in for a sweet, quick kiss that surprises us both. "Thank you. I won't be long."

"Take as much time as you want."

"Okay. I'm gonna go change and get my board."

He starts up the trail, then stops and comes back for one more kiss. This one is deeper and sends little waves of warmth all through me.

He pulls back a little, rests his forehead on mine, so we're eye to eye. Smiles. "Okay. I really am gonna go change."

"Okay," I echo. "I'll be here."

He takes a few steps backward, keeping his eyes on me until he has to turn around. I watch as he jogs up the trail to his bus, wanting him to come back and kiss me again, knowing that if he does, I won't be able to hold back anymore.

By the time he does come back with his surfboard, I've found my way down to another little wooden platform, midway between flights of stairs, complete with a bench, a railing, and a perfect view of the waterfall in the cove below.

"I brought you a sweatshirt," Colton says, handing it to me. "Just in case." He leans in for another quick kiss, then bounds down the stairs in his rash guard and trunks, board under one arm, and it makes me happy inside to see him this way. The lightness is back in his step.

I stand at the railing for a moment and watch as he throws his board into the deep blue of the water, jumps onto it, and starts paddling with the grace and ease of someone who never spent a single day away from it. You'd never know it'd been any other way for him. You'd never know any of it from the outside.

A tall wave rises up in front of him, and I get nervous, like I would if it were me out there, but Colton digs his arms in and paddles hard, then pushes the nose of the board down just as the wave pitches forward and begins to break. For the briefest moment I can see his silhouette in the face of it, the light shining through the water, and it's so beautiful it makes me want to cry at the impossibility of this situation I've created.

A cool breeze swirls up from the water, carrying on it

a chill, and the slightest hint of rain. It rolls over my bare skin, and I pull the sweatshirt around me as he finishes out the wave and turns to paddle for another one. There's a flash out on the horizon, so quick I wonder if I saw it at all, but a few moments later I hear the low, telling rumble of thunder. The clouds have moved in closer already, trailing faint gray streaks down to the water, starting to crowd the sun that was so bright only moments before.

Colton catches the next wave just as another flash of lightning zags the sky. This time only a few beats pass before the rumble of thunder follows again. I can see white-caps begin to form out on the water as the wind picks up. I expect Colton to paddle in, but he turns his board around and heads back out toward the building surf. A fat drop of rain lands on my cheek, and I wipe it away. I look out at the water, at Colton paddling his board against the backdrop of the stormy sky, and I wish he'd come in. Lightning flashes again, and he sits up and turns toward the shore. He waves from the water, nods like he's okay, and then raises a single finger, like "one more."

I wave back, and raindrops begin to fall, one after another, dotting the staircase all around me and adding a new layer to the air. Another flash of lightning zips across the sky, then a crack of thunder opens it up. I yank the hood over my head and squint through the downpour as Colton goes for a wave and catches it. As soon as he finishes out the ride, he paddles the rest of the way in; and when he gets to the beach, he stands up and waves again, then tucks his board under his arm.

Colton hits the beach running as the thunder booms above us. He yells something to me, but his words are lost in the wind. The rain pours down in a steady sheet, creating little pinpricks of cold all over my face and bare legs, soaking through the sweatshirt fast.

When Colton reaches me, he lets out a whoop, and I can't help but laugh at how I must look standing there, the rain plastering my hair to my cheeks. "C'mon," he yells above the storm and the surf. He grabs my hand and pulls me toward the stairs, motioning for me to go first, in front of him. I take the stairs two at a time, driven hard by the rain, and the cold, and the fact that he's right behind me. Another flash of lightning makes me scream, and I feel the boom of the accompanying thunder clap in my chest. Colton laughs out loud from behind me. "Go, go, go!"

By the time we get to the top of the stairs, the dirt trail has become a small, rushing river, and my flip-flops slip with every step I take. Colton's bus sits beside the fence, a bright-turquoise splash in the gray blur of rain. I climb up over the little ladder with Colton right behind me. The rain pounds loud on the roof of the bus and almost drowns out the sound of the door when I slide it open. We tumble in, Colton right after me, and he slams the door closed behind us, all in one motion.

For a second it seems like the volume has been turned down, but then the sky unleashes another torrent of rain, this one even louder than the last. I lean against the seat to catch my breath, and Colton scoots himself back next to me to catch his. We're quiet a moment before we both burst out laughing. Colton shakes the water out of his hair, and I wring it from mine and pinch his soaked sweatshirt away from my chest.

"That was crazy," he says, still out of breath. "That came out of nowhere."

"No, it didn't. I could see it coming, all the way in. I've never seen anything like it. I thought you were gonna get hit by lightning out there."

"I kinda did too," he admits. "Nothing like a little brush with death to remind you you're alive." He smiles, then reaches behind him and grabs two towels. Hands me one.

He runs his over his hair first, and I do the same before I peel off the wet sweatshirt and drape it over the back of the driver's seat. Another flash-boom erupts outside, and the rain pounds harder in answer. I wrap the towel around my shoulders and pull it tight; then we sit there on the bed, our backs leaned against the wall, catching our breaths and watching the rain streak down the windows.

"Looks like we may be camping out here after all, the way it's coming down out there," Colton says, glancing over at me with a smile. "We didn't even make it to the waterfall."

"No shooting stars or s'mores either."

"I know," Colton says, shaking his head. "All I've got is"—he leans over me and rummages around in the center console—"half a bottle of water, four pieces of gum, and two Rolos. I don't know how we're gonna survive." He does his best to put on a serious expression, but the corner of his mouth twitches up. He shivers.

"We should get these wet clothes off," I say, conscious now of the cold.

A smile breaks over Colton's face. He raises an eyebrow. "Yeah?"

I laugh. "That came out wrong. Sort of. I meant—"

Colton just keeps smiling as heat floods my cheeks and I try again. "I meant because of the cold, because we're wet, and you can get . . ."

He laughs softly and reaches out, tucks a damp strand of hair behind my ear. And in that tiny moment when his fingers brush my skin, there is an unmistakable shift in the air between us. The rain falls in a steady hush, a soft-gray curtain that blurs everything beyond the space where we sit, and I lean into him.

Colton's arms come around me and lift me onto his lap

so we're facing each other. The towel slides from my shoulders, and a shiver runs through me, but I don't feel cold. I only feel the heat of his hands as they slide up my back, into the wet tangles of my hair, and travel down over my neck and shoulders, leaving a trail of tiny sparks everywhere they touch. I kiss him, and he tastes like the ocean and the rain, and everything I want in that moment.

Thunder booms low and distant, and I feel a wave of need rise up in us both as our lips come together with more urgency. Our bodies follow, pressing against each other, wanting and needing to be closer. Colton shrugs off his towel, and my lips move to his neck as I run my hands down his chest to his stomach, where they trail along the edge of his trunks.

He pulls me into him like a reflex and finds my mouth again as I find the edge of my tank top. I peel the wet fabric away from my skin and pull it over my head, and the coolness of the air sends another shiver through me as I reach back and find the hook of my bra.

When I let it slide down my arms and drop to the floor, I feel the sudden inhale it causes in Colton. His hands come to my face, and he presses his forehead against mine, breathing hard. Out of focus. Eye to eye.

I hear the rain on the roof again. Feel my heart, pounding in my chest, and our breaths, shaky and uneven.

Colton pulls back the slightest bit and brushes his thumb

over my tiny scar from the day we met. I close my eyes as he kisses it. He breathes in deep, then leans back, and when I open my eyes, he's reaching for his rash guard. He pauses, just barely, then pulls it up over his head, and we sit facing each other.

Bare, in the soft light.

My breath catches as my eyes travel away from his, down to his chest, to the part of himself he's kept hidden away for so long.

The scar starts just above the notch where his collarbones meet and cuts a thin, clean line down the center of his chest. I can feel him watching me take it in, feel him waiting to see what I'll do, and in that moment, the need to reach out, to touch him, is overwhelming. I raise my hand, but hesitate in the space between us, not sure if it's okay.

Without saying a word, he takes my hand in his and guides it to the center of his chest. Presses it against his skin so I can feel the pounding there that echoes my own.

"Quinn . . ."

My name is a whisper that pulls me to him, to a place where there's only us, only now.

I let myself fall back onto the bed, pulling him on top of me until I can feel the full weight of his body pressed into mine.

His lips trail down my neck, brush soft over my collarbones, then come back to my mouth, and we kiss away our pasts. We kiss away everything that isn't us, here, now. Our scars, and our pains, and our secrets, and our guilt. We give them to each other and take them from each other until they all fade away in the rhythm of the rain.

And breath.

And heartbeats.

"There are moments in life, when the heart is so full
of emotion
That if by chance it be shaken, or into its depths like
a pebble
Drops some careless word, it overflows, and its secret,
Spilt on the ground like water, can never be gathered
together."

—Henry Wadsworth Longfellow,
"The Courtship of Miles Standish"

CHAPTER TWENTY-NINE

I WAKE SLOWLY, so the only thing I'm aware of at first is a low, steady sound, and the rhythmic rise and fall of the place where I lay my head. I'm wrapped in warmth, but just beyond its edge is a current of rain-drenched air that makes me want to tuck myself closer to Colton, and the heat of his skin, and the beat of his heart.

For a brief moment the thought surprises me. For so long I thought of him as having Trent's heart. I can't say when it happened, or how it changed in my mind, but now that thought feels distant. Untrue even. This sound that I can hear and feel—it's Colton's heart. I open my eyes, and when

I see the curve of his chin, the tan of his arm wrapped around me, it comes back in a warm rush, the memory of his soft lips pressed to me as the rain beat down insistently. That was his heart and mine together; those moments were ours alone.

Pale light filters in through the fogged windows, and I can still hear the soft hush of drizzle outside, punctuated by the sound of bigger drops from the cypress we're parked under, as they land on the metal roof of the bus.

I bring my hand to the center of his chest, trace a delicate finger down his neck, and Colton stirs at my touch. He takes in a deep breath and covers my hand with his like he did before. Pulls it to his chest and smiles without opening his eyes.

"Hi," I say, all of a sudden feeling a little shy, with our bodies still tangled under a blanket.

Colton cracks one eye open and then the other, and tilts his chin down so he can look at me. "So I didn't dream it." A smile spreads over his face. "Well. Not this time anyway."

I laugh, give him a playful shove, but the flashes of us, with the rain all around, and the idea of him thinking of me that way send a whole new rush of warmth through me. I pull myself up to his lips, and his arms come around me; and just as everything is about to disappear again, I hear the buzz of my cell phone.

I start to reach for it, to see who it is, but Colton pulls

me back into him and mumbles into my lips as he kisses me, "Don't worry 'bout that right now." I kiss him back as the phone continues to buzz before falling silent. Then there's the short beep of a voicemail. A tiny worry tugs at me from the corner of my mind. I told Ryan I was going to see Colton. Maybe she's just checking in.

Normally, I wouldn't think much of it; but the storm— and the fact that I'm not where I said I'd be and it's getting late—makes me anxious enough to pull away from Colton, pull the blanket to my chest, and reach for my phone.

When I see the home screen, my stomach drops.

Twelve missed calls.

Mom. Ryan. Gran.

Over and over.

"Oh god."

Colton sits up, alert all of a sudden. "What?" he asks. "What's the matter?"

I fumble with the phone, try to pull up the first voice-mail. "I . . . I don't know, I think maybe, maybe it's—"

Ryan's voice, urgent in my ear, cuts me off. "Quinn, it's Dad. You need to get to the hospital now."

The ER doors whoosh open. Along with a pungent, antiseptic smell, a flash of the last time I was here in *this* hospital—over a year ago—hits me with a force I'm not prepared for. I was a wreck in my running clothes, still holding Trent's shoe, my dad at the nurses' desk asking questions, Trent's parents' faces when they saw me. He'd already been moved from the ER. Decisions had been made. Papers signed. The chaplain had been sent. Good-byes said without me.

I stop, try to breathe, but the floor feels unsteady beneath me.

"Whoa," Colton says, grabbing my elbow. "You all right?"

I open my mouth to answer, but the sight of my family stops me. They sit in the same beige chairs I sat in with my dad, waiting to see Trent. Waiting to say good-bye.

Now it's Gran, Mom, and Ryan who sit tense, without talking. Mom stares into the middle distance, a stricken look on her face, like she's failed—as if she's running through her mind all the things she could've done differently. Ryan, who's dressed in her painting clothes and looking like she's on the edge of tears, focuses on some unseen spot on the ground, like if she concentrates on it hard enough, no tears will fall. And Gran. She sits very straight, and very still, purse in her lap, hands folded over it, calm in a silent storm.

Colton's hand moves gently to my back. "Is that your family?"

I nod, bracing myself for the word *stroke*. And then I cross the ER to where the bank of chairs is. When I get to it, Ryan is the first to look up, and her eyes widen when she sees us. It's only then that I realize what I must look like, with my hair tangled and wavy around my face, mascara smeared, Colton's still-damp sweatshirt hanging on me.

"What happened—is Dad okay?" I feel the tears readying themselves for whatever the answers to those questions may be. "Did he have a stroke?"

Mom stands up and pulls me into a hug so tight, I wonder if it's worse than I imagined. After a long moment she loosens her grip but doesn't let go. "We don't know for sure yet. They're evaluating him now, and we'll know more soon."

"What happened? How did this . . . I thought he was . . ."

I don't finish, because I realize I haven't thought anything about it for the last few weeks: his medications, or his checkups. Symptoms. I just assumed he was okay. Safe.

I let myself forget there's no such thing.

"He was helping me with one of my canvases," Ryan says from her seat without looking up from the floor. "And he just—he just sounded funny all of a sudden, and I thought he was joking, so I laughed." She looks at me now, tears in her eyes. "I laughed, and then his eyes rolled back into his head, and he just fell down. He just fell. . . ." She wrings her hands in her lap.

Gran puts her hand on top of Ryan's, firmly enough to still them. "And then you acted, and you called 911, and that's all you could've done."

Now Ryan sits up. "No, I should've seen it right away, I should've called sooner—"

Mom steps in now, won't let Ryan blame herself. "You did all any of us could've done, sweetheart. The rest was beyond what any of us could control."

I don't think my mom believes her own words. I can see it again—her going over all the preventive measures she should've forced on my dad—and it makes me want to reach out and tell her that she couldn't have. That sometimes, no matter how much we regret or wish things were different, there is nothing we can do to make it so.

Colton clears his throat and shifts on his feet next to me. Gran is the only one other than me who notices.

"Quinn, you haven't yet introduced us to your friend." She nods in my direction, and worry spreads all through me.

Colton steps forward, hand extended to Gran. "I'm Colton."

Gran takes his hand in both of hers. "So pleased to meet you, Colton. You must be the reason Quinn has become so enthralled with the ocean. I can see why," she says with a wink. "This is my daughter, Susan, and Quinn's sister, Ryan."

"Nice to meet you both," Colton says.

My mom nods and smiles politely. Ryan stands and shakes his hand, then looks from him to me and back again. "I've heard a lot about you," she says. I give her a look she doesn't see, because she seems to be studying Colton.

She glances at me, and I silently plead with her not to say anything more.

"Good things," she says, getting it. "Thank you for coming with her."

"Of course," Colton answers.

We stand there for a long moment, silent, until a tired-looking doctor in scrubs approaches, clipboard in hand.

"Mrs. Sullivan?"

"Yes?" Mom says, standing up.

We hold our collective breath as the doctor takes in the group of us standing there. "May I speak freely? About your husband?"

Mom nods.

"Okay," he says. "The good news is that your husband is stable, he did not suffer a stroke, and there is no permanent damage."

We all nod like we understand; then we wait for the bad news.

"The bad news is that this is his second TIA, and that his scans show a small clot forming in his carotid artery, which leads to the brain. If left untreated, it's likely that he *will* suffer a stroke—or worse—in the near future. We have a few options, but time is of the essence, and I'd like to get him into surgery as soon as possible."

Mom nods, taking it in, as we all are. "Can I see him?"

"Of course," the doctor says. "Come with me."

She glances, just briefly, at all of us, and Gran makes a shooing motion at her. "Go. We'll be here."

Gran's not even finished saying it before Mom has turned to walk down the hall with the doctor. I can see that her focus has completely shifted from us, and I don't blame her. We've disappeared, and right now her world is my dad. I think of the two of them, of all their history together—thirty-six years' worth—and how I felt about losing Trent after just a fraction of that. How it would feel to lose Colton now. I'm sure it's different for her because of all that time, but it's terrifying to realize how much of your world is wrapped around loving another person.

Ryan falls back into her seat, relieved, but not completely. "I can't believe I laughed at him. I just . . . It happened so fast, I didn't realize."

Gran turns to her, her voice soft. "Come on now; that's done and past, and you need to let that go." She takes Ryan's hand. "Let's you and me take a walk."

Ryan's arm hangs limply from Gran's hand, and she shakes her head and takes in another shuddery breath.

"Get up," Gran says, with a little force behind it this time.

That gets my sister's attention, and a tiny moment of understanding passes between the two of them, Ryan hearing the words she said to Gran so long ago echoed back at her. She swallows hard. Nods and then obeys. Gran turns her eyes on me and Colton. "You two'll be all right here?"

"Yes," I say, though I'm not sure it's true.

"Good. We won't be long." And with that, she puts an arm around Ryan's shoulder and steers her down the hall to the door, and out into the cloudy twilight.

I finally exhale.

Colton sits next to me. "That was scary, huh?" He rests his hand on my knee. "Sounds like your dad's gonna be okay, though."

"I wish there were a guarantee," I say, looking over at him.

He presses his lips together. "There never is. For any of us. But that's the way life is."

We're quiet a moment.

"You hungry?" Colton asks. "Thirsty? Want coffee or hot chocolate or something? I know how to find my way around a hospital." He smiles, and I can't believe how easy these little references to being sick come out, now that I know. Almost like he's relieved to have his secret out in the open.

"Just a bottle of water maybe?" I say weakly.

"You got it." Colton gets to his feet quickly, happy to be of service, but then he bends down in front of me, tilts my chin upward so I'm looking right at him and he's looking right at me, and starts to say something, but then he just kisses me gently on the forehead. "Quinn, I . . . I'll be right back."

He turns and heads down another hallway, and I lean back into my chair, put my hands in the sweatshirt pockets, and close my eyes to take a minute and breathe. I try to wrap my mind around what happened to my dad, and what the doctor said, and the likelihood that everything will be okay. But all I see is Colton, there in the pale storm light, my hand on his bare chest, his lips on mine, the rain all around us like a dream.

I open my eyes, and the fluorescent hospital glow chases it all away.

A few minutes pass, and I fidget with something tucked deep in the corner of Colton's pocket for a few seconds before I wonder what it is and pull it out. It's a piece of paper, folded down into a small, tight square.

I start to unfold it without even thinking but stop dead when I recognize the tattered, cream-colored stationery. My heart drops right through the bottom of my chest. All my guilt and secrets come rushing back at me from the thing in my hands. Like punishment for what I've done. I don't have to open the letter to know what it says. I wrote draft after draft, night after night, until I felt I'd gotten it exactly right. Until it said exactly what I wanted to say to the person who had Trent's heart.

Nausea rolls through my stomach as I unfold it slowly, careful not to tear the once-thick paper that's been worn down by more than just the storm. My eyes run over the words, over my handwriting, over the creases that aren't mine, creases from being folded and unfolded, over and over again. The ones Colton must've made to fit it into his pocket. To carry it around with him.

I look down at the words, my words, so full of grief and sadness. The person who wrote that letter feels like a stranger. She was someone who was looking for a way to hold on to Trent. Someone who didn't think she could love anyone else. Who didn't know that the person she was writing to would be the one to prove her wrong.

"What're you doing with that?"

Colton's voice snaps my head up, and the look of shock on his face must mirror my own.

His eyes are glued to the letter in my hands.

"I . . ." I fumble to fold it back up, but he sets the two steaming cups of coffee on the floor and takes it from me before I can. His sudden intensity startles me.

"I'm sorry," I say. "I didn't mean— It was in your pocket, and I thought maybe it was—"

"It's not yours to read," Colton says, and I don't know what's worse: his tone, or the awful irony of his words.

I look at him standing there, trying to fold it back into the small rectangle that was tucked down in his pocket for who knows how long, and I can't do it anymore. Can't stand that I've kept this secret for so long. Finally, I find the words. I say them carefully, so there's no mistaking them.

"It *is* mine."

His hands freeze in the air. He looks at me, confused. *"What?"*

There's a quaver in his voice that makes me not want to say what comes next, but I have to.

"It's my letter." I swallow hard, my mouth all of a sudden dry. "I wrote it."

"You *what*?"

I try to keep my voice even. Wish there were more air in this room. "I wrote that letter," I say. "To you. Months ago, after . . ." My voice breaks. "After my boyfriend was killed in an accident."

These words, and all the truth in them, are made of air, barely audible, but he hears them, and every muscle in his body tenses. He shakes his head.

"Before I knew you," I add, with the unreasonable hope that somehow that'll make a difference; but I know as soon as I look at Colton that it doesn't.

He stands there silent, and statue still, except for the tiny motion of his jaw tightening.

I stand up, take a step toward him. "Colton, *please*—"

He backs away. "Did you know?" he asks, his voice cold. "When we met. Did you know who I was?"

The question sends a hot flood of tears to my eyes. "Yes," I whisper.

Colton turns to go.

"Wait," I plead. "*Please*. Let me just explain—"

He stops. Whips back around to face me. "Explain *what*? That you went looking for the person who got your boyfriend's heart? That you found me after I signed a paper that said I didn't want to be found?" Anger flashes over his face like the lightning over the ocean. "Or that you sat there next to me a few *hours* ago while I told you everything, and you said nothing?" He pauses, and something else flashes over his face. Maybe the memory of what came after that. But it's gone just as quickly, and his voice goes hollow. "Which part did you want to explain?"

I open my mouth to answer, but the truth of what I've done leaves me speechless for a moment. And then I give the only explanation I can come up with.

"You never wrote back."

I say it to the floor, not an accusation, but the explanation for it all, in its most simple, honest form.

Colton takes a step toward me. "And why do you think? I never wanted this. I never wanted any of this." He looks directly into my eyes, and I swear I don't recognize him at all. "Do me a favor," he says. "Forget you knew me. Because I *never* should've known you."

And then he's gone. Through the automatic doors, out into the night.

Broken Heart Syndrome

*"Broken heart syndrome is a condition in which
extreme stress can lead to heart muscle failure. The
failure is severe, but often short-term....The cause of
broken heart syndrome is not fully known. In most
cases, symptoms are triggered by extreme emotional or
physical stress, such as intense grief, anger, or surprise.
Researchers think that the stress releases hormones that
'stun' the heart and affect its ability to pump blood to
the body."*

—*The National Heart, Lung, and Blood Institute*

CHAPTER THIRTY

I SIT IN the waiting room chair in a haze. I can't move. My
chest is caving in.

Faceless people come and go past the chairs where I sit.
Garbled voices speak over the intercom. Gran is on one
side of me, one hand tapping the armrest, the other resting on my knee. Ryan is on the other side. She doesn't
look at me, doesn't say a word, and I'm not sure if it's
because she's worrying about Dad or because she's just as

267

horrified by me as I am.

I am a horrible, selfish, lying person.

We wait, together in those chairs, but in our own separate worlds. A doctor comes to give us an update. Dad's just been taken to surgery. Settle in. It'll be a few hours. Mom comes back to us quiet, lips pressed together to maintain control. She looks small standing there in front of us. And so scared. It's heart wrenching and terrifying at the same time.

Gran gets up and wraps her arms around Mom. "It's going to be all right." She can't know for sure. None of us can, but we all cling to the sureness in Gran's voice.

Mom nods into her shoulder, and her lip trembles. Her eyes well up, but when she sees Ryan and me, something shifts in her. She meets Gran's eyes, and Gran releases her from the embrace. Mom wipes her own eyes, straightens up, and opens her arms for us to come to her. Becomes as strong and sure as she can for us as she repeats Gran's words.

"It's going to be all right."

We all sit in a row: Gran, Ryan, Mom, me. We're quiet as we wait, weighted with worry, but pulled closer by the strength we draw from one another. Eventually, exhaustion overcomes them. Gran falls asleep with her cheek propped on her fist. Ryan moves to an empty row of chairs and stretches out over them, and falls asleep the second she closes her eyes. Mom's chin drops to her chest.

And then I am alone again.

My eyes burn, and my body aches for sleep, but my mind won't allow it. The scene with Colton plays again and again in my mind as the clock ticks away the hours like a heart-beat. His hurt and anger, my guilt and shame. Secrets. Lies. Wounds that can't be helped or treated. Damage that is irreversible.

I don't know how much time has passed when the doctor appears in front of us. I put a hand on my mom's shoul-der, and she sits up immediately, blinking in the fluorescent light. The lines around her eyes are deep, but when she sees the doctor, she stands, alert.

He smiles. "The news is good." Ryan and Gran are both up now too, and they join us around the doctor. "Surgery went smoothly, and we were able to remove the clot and place the stent. He's up in recovery now."

Mom hugs the doctor. "Thank you, thank you so much."

His smile is sincere but tired as he pats her back. "He's not awake yet, but I can have a nurse take you up so you're there when the anesthesia wears off."

When the doctor leaves us, a nurse comes to take Mom to Dad, and Gran decides she'll stay and wait but that Ryan and I should go home. We don't argue with her, and we don't say anything as we walk down the hall, but we both seem to breathe the same sigh of relief. It only lasts a second for me, though. We walk out the same doors Colton did, and now there's even more room in me to feel the full weight of what sent him through them. Guilt comes in like air with the next breath I take, and my heart and lungs carry it through every part of me.

I wonder where he is. *Come back,* I think. *Be here.* But I know he won't.

The distant whine of a siren gets louder and closer as we cross the parking lot to Ryan's car. She clicks the remote key and opens her door. I watch the ambulance pull in under the Emergency sign. The siren stops, but the lights keep spinning, blue-red, blue-red as the side doors open and medics climb out on both sides.

Blue and red lights, swirling against the pale sunrise sky. The clipped voices of the medics, the loud jumble of their radios in the background.

I can't breathe all of a sudden.

"Quinn," Ryan says, but her voice sounds faraway.

I'm there on our road, on my knees, losing everything all over again.

The back doors of the ambulance burst open, and another medic climbs out, then reaches in and pulls the end of a gurney. Calls to the others, "Get him in there! Let's go, let's go!"

"Quinn, let's *go*." Ryan's voice snaps me back here, to the present, but it doesn't hurt any less.

Here, I've lost even more.

"Go to your bosom; knock there, and ask your heart what it doth know."

—*William Shakespeare,* Measure for Measure

CHAPTER THIRTY-ONE

I SIT ON my bed, staring at my phone in my hand. At Colton's number, ready to be dialed if I just hit the call button. But I don't. I know he won't answer. I've called, again and again, and now it just goes straight to voicemail, like he turned off his phone, or threw it away. I've thought about going to him, tried to imagine what words I could say that might make him understand, but there are none. I try to picture if we could go back in time. Try to see us out on the water together, or at that cove with the waterfall, or watching the sunset from the beach. But I can't do that either. All I can see is his face, so angry, and hear the words he said to me, in a voice that sounded like a stranger's.

Forget you knew me.

It wasn't anger I heard in those words. It was hurt. Caused by me. No one can tell me it was an accident, or that it was beyond my control, or that I couldn't have done anything differently.

I searched for him. I found him. I let myself fall in love with him.

I had no right to do any of those things.

They were choices I made, but in making them, I took away his, and like Ryan said, I took away any chance that we had for something real. I erased all our moments, and days, and experiences before they even existed. And now I'm the past that he wants to forget. I have no choice but to let him.

I retreat into the isolation of my own past, where I deserve to be. Where I am alone with all the things I wish I could change. I don't sleep. Don't eat. I tell Ryan what happened when I went to his shop to tell him the truth, and then about the storm, and the hospital. After that I hardly speak. She gives me my space. Runs by herself. Doesn't ask questions or offer advice. I can't tell if it's because I don't ask for any or if she has none for this.

A couple days later, when Dad comes home from the hospital, I pull myself out of my room to let him know how relieved I am that he's okay. How much I love him. I try to help take care of him, but I'm only half there. Ryan, still shaken from witnessing his attack, hovers around him, giving him hugs and getting teary out of nowhere. Mom manages his recovery: doctors' orders, prescriptions, covering for him at the office. I fade into the background, sinking lower and lower.

Losing myself again.

I'm sitting at my computer in the same pajamas I've worn for the last two days, scrolling up and down Shelby's blog, when Ryan comes in without knocking. She sees the picture of Colton on the screen before I can close the window.

"Still nothing?"

I shake my head.

"Why don't you call him?"

"I have. Lots of times. He won't answer."

She presses her lips together and nods. "I guess I probably wouldn't either, if I were him. Not after finding out like that."

I don't feel like talking about it, so I don't say anything. Ryan takes a deep breath and leans against the desk in front of me.

"I got in," she says.

"What?"

"To that art school, in Italy. They loved my portfolio. Apparently, heartbreak makes for compelling art."

"That's really great," I say. But it doesn't sound convincing. The thought of not having her here chokes me up. "When do you leave?"

"In a couple of weeks." We're quiet a moment, and though I know it's what she wants, she seems a little sad too. "I'm gonna miss you," she says. "And I'm worried about you."

"I can't stand me right now."

"You know how I said he deserves to know the truth?"

I glance up at her.

"Well, he does, Quinn. He deserves to know every-thing—not just what he thinks he knows."

"What are you talking about?" I ask.

"I'm talking the rest of the truth. That it started out being about Trent, but somewhere along the line that changed. That you fell in love with *him*. That you were scared. That you didn't want to hurt him or lose him. Those things are all the truth too, aren't they?"

My eyes well up, and I look at my sister. "He told me to forget I *knew* him." I swallow over the lump in my throat, and my voice comes out thick with tears. "He doesn't want to hear anything I have to say."

"Are you kidding me? Those are the things he *needs* to hear you say. You think *he's* not hurting right now, walking around knowing half the truth?"

Tears, one after another, roll silently down my cheeks at the thought.

"Think of all the things you've ever regretted not doing or saying. All the things you've wished you could change." She shakes her head. "You, of all people, know how much those things can sting. You know how long they can stay with you, and change you." She pauses and takes a long look at the picture of Colton on my computer screen. When she brings her eyes back to mine, they are serious.

"So don't let them. Do something. Go find him and tell him."

"Give all to love;
Obey thy heart."

—*Ralph Waldo Emerson*

CHAPTER THIRTY-TWO

I PULL OFF in the same overlook I did the first time I made this drive to see Colton. Sunshine and salt air pour in when I roll down the window, and I try to breathe, just like I did that day. My hands shake just the same at the thought of seeing him.

But so much is different.

Then, I drove over promising myself I wouldn't speak to him, that I would be invisible. That I wouldn't interfere in his life. Now I need him to listen. I want him to *see* me. And in spite of what led me to him, I don't want to think of him not being a part of my life.

I need to tell him the truth that got tangled up in the lies. How I went looking for Trent's heart, for a connection to the past. A way to hold on. But that what I found when I found him was a reason to let go. I need to tell him I wouldn't change that, not even if I could.

♥ ♥ ♥

By the time I turn onto Main Street, I am a mess. Even more now than on that first day. I park in the same place I did that day, in front of the café, and peek in the window to see if there's a chance I could catch him in there again, but it's empty. I take a deep breath and cross the street to Good Clean Fun, eyes down, trying to gather my courage as I go. When I step onto the curb and finally look up, the ground disappears from beneath my feet.

The store is dark inside. The racks that are normally filled with kayaks sit empty, and in front of the closed door, there are bunches of flowers and signs.

Signs with Colton's name on them.

My eyes go blurry, and all the air in the world is gone. I take a step toward the door, but I can't even see it. All I can see is the hospital, and Colton's face, and the way he looked when I told him the truth. The way he looked when he left. The way he didn't look back.

I crumple right where I'm standing, like I don't have legs beneath me.

This can't be happening.

Not when I haven't even—when I haven't gotten a chance to tell him, or set things right, or just . . . just *see* him.

My head falls to my knees, and I weep. Weep for myself, and for Colton, and for Trent too. It's too much, this. Life, and love, and how fragile it all is. It repeats, over and over in my head, a sad, desperate refrain.

This can't be happening, this can't be happening, this can't—

"Quinn? Is that you?"

It takes a second for the voice to register, but when it does, I lift my head slowly, afraid of what I'll see when I look at Shelby. She's standing above me, and I have to squint through the sunlight and my tears to see her. She looks at me, then at the flowers and signs in front of the door, and her eyes widen.

"Oh my god," she says. Then she sits down in front of me and takes my hands in hers. "He's not— This is— He's going to be okay."

"What?" The word barely comes out.

"Colton. He's going to be okay. People just keep bringing stuff here because he can't really have any visitors yet, and I had to close the shop until my parents can get back."

Relief opens up my chest, and I can finally, fully look at her. She has the same green eyes as him—kind, and soulful, but weary in a way too.

I wipe at my own eyes. "What happened?"

"He went into acute rejection four days ago."

"Oh my god."

My own heart practically stops, and guilt wraps itself tight around me. Four days ago. Four days ago when we drove off from the shop after his fight with Shelby about missing his meds, and when we spent the afternoon together, and when not once did I see him swallow a pill.

Four days ago when he found out the truth.

"It was really scary," she says. "I knew something was wrong when he got home. He went to his room, and I heard glass breaking, and when I ran in, he was smashing all those bottles." She pauses like she's seeing it again.

"I ran in and tried to get him to stop, but he wouldn't until they were all gone; and he wouldn't talk to me, wouldn't tell me what was wrong. Said he just wanted to be left alone. A few hours later he was having trouble breathing, and he looked awful. He was almost in full failure by the time the ambulance got to the house the next morning."

"Oh my god," I whisper. My eyes well up, and I look down at my hands twisting in my lap. *It's my fault, it's my fault, it's my fault.*

"He's stable now, but not out of the woods. They have him on heavy doses of antirejection meds, and he'll have to be monitored at the hospital until his biopsies are clear."

Shelby takes a deep breath and leans back against the wall. "He's not responding as well as they'd like, though, and I think . . . I think there's more to it than just him missing a few doses of his meds." She looks at me then. "He told me what happened—with the letter."

Every muscle in me tenses, bracing for what she thinks of me.

"Which is why I didn't call when all this happened. I

hated what you did. When he told me, I wanted to hate *you* for taking away his personal choice in the matter."

I flinch, and she pauses. Softens a little.

"But then I realized I've been doing the same thing for a while now, just in a different way. Putting it all out there for everyone to see, because somehow it made me feel better. But Colton didn't really want that either."

I don't know what to say.

Shelby looks me in the eye. "I was wrong to do that," she says. "And you were wrong to do what you did." She takes another deep breath, and I fumble for the right words to apologize.

"But honestly?" she says. "He's been better than I've ever seen him since he met you. I never wrote about it, but he really struggled after his transplant—with a lot of things we didn't know how to help him with. I wasn't sure we'd ever get the old Colton back." She smiles. "But then he met you, and it was like he came alive again. I don't know if I've ever seen my brother as happy as he was when he was with you. So if there's anything to blame you for, it's that."

Hot tears streak down my cheeks—happy and sad and grateful all at once.

Shelby smiles. "You were the first person he asked for when he woke up, and I didn't want— I didn't think it was a good idea for him to see you." She takes my hand in hers and squeezes. "But he's having a hard time right now, and I think he *needs* to see you, so it's good you're here. I can take you over there."

I nod, still unable to speak through my tears. I felt like I knew Shelby from following her updates on Colton's page, and then I thought I knew her better from the few times I met her, but in this moment I can see her for who she truly is: a caring, fiercely protective, kindhearted person who would do anything for her brother, including forgive me.

"Thank you," I finally manage.

She squeezes my hand again. "Thank *you*, for finding my brother."

"Bring your secrets, bring your scars . . .
Unpack your heart"
— Phillip Phillips, *"Unpack Your Heart"*

CHAPTER THIRTY-THREE

"GO AHEAD," SHELBY says when I hesitate outside the door of Colton's hospital room. "He'll be happy to see you when he wakes up." She hands me a bag, and the bunches of flowers and signs from the store. "Here. You can bring him these."

I scoop it all into my arms. Wish I'd brought something of my own to give him.

"I'll be in the reception room if you need me, okay?"

I nod, my heart in my throat. "Thank you."

I watch as she walks down the hall, and when she turns the corner, it's just me outside his door. I glance at the clipboard in the rack with the neon-yellow sticker that says *Thomas, Colton,* and the attached charts and scribbled notes that I don't understand. Seeing his name like that makes it real, but that's nothing compared to the second I step through the doorway and see him there in the hospital bed, so many tubes and monitors hooked up to him. It's an image I've seen before, but it's so different now that I know him. So much sharper.

I step closer.

His chest rises and falls at a slow, steady pace, and the beeping of the monitors is reassuring. I walk over to the one that looks like a TV, where a constant line spools out across the screen, jumping with each beat, visual proof that his heart is still working. I close my eyes and say a silent thank-you to Trent, and though the circumstances seem strange and incomprehensible, it feels right.

I know Colton wouldn't like me to see him this way, and I don't want to disturb him, so I just stand there at first, not knowing what to do. I think of all the things I want to say to him, all the truths I hope he hears, and the things I hope he feels too.

I set the bag on the floor next to the chair and put the vase of flowers on the side table as softly as I can. I watch the monitor. I watch him breathe. His hand hangs, just barely, off the side of the bed, and I want to reach out and take it in mine. Press it to my own heart so he can know what's really there.

I stand next to the bed for a moment longer, then sit down in the chair to wait. Colton stirs at the sound. His eyes open just a crack, and then all the way when he sees me.

"You're here," he says. His voice is hoarse, weak, and I

have to fight the urge to wrap my arms around him and kiss a thousand apologies over him.

"Hi," I whisper, afraid to do anything more. I feel more bare in this moment than I did in the rain with him that afternoon.

He clears his throat and pulls himself up a bit. Winces, then reaches out his hand, and I'm there in a second, taking it in mine, and all the words I've been waiting to say come tumbling out, one right on top of another.

"I'm so sorry, for all of this, for everything. I just wanted to see who you were. I wasn't even going to talk to you. But then you walked in, and everything changed. And when you showed up at my door with that flower, and took me out on the water, and in the cave, and . . . every day, you showed me so much, and it got harder and harder, and I just couldn't . . ."

I pause, take in a shaky breath, don't bother to wipe the tears sliding down my cheeks.

"I couldn't tell you because I never expected to fall in love, but I did. With you. I did, and I am, and I know it was wrong how it happened and that you might not ever forgive me, but I—"

"Quinn, stop," he says, his voice rough.

My hands fall at my sides, and I take a step back, terrified that none of what I just said matters. He doesn't look at me. Just keeps his eyes focused on the empty space between us.

We're silent for a long moment, one that's made even longer by the beeping of the monitors and the gathering dread in my chest.

Finally, he looks at me, but his eyes are hard to read. "I don't—" He stops. Takes a deep breath. "None of that matters to me."

He looks away, and my heart falls.

"Not like you think. It did at first, when you told me. I didn't know how to handle it, so I didn't. I just reacted, because I hated that you were the one who wrote that letter." He looks at me now, eyes full of regret, and I don't know if I can take what's coming next.

"But I've been lying here in this bed for the last three days, and all I've been thinking is how much more I hate it that I was the one you thought didn't write back."

"What?" I take a step toward him. "That doesn't matter to me anymore, that was—"

"It does matter," Colton says, "because I did write you back."

"I don't understand."

"I wrote you back," he says quietly. "So many times."

"What do you . . . ?"

He pulls himself up to a sitting position, and his eyes find the bag that Shelby asked me to bring in. "Hand me that?"

I do, and with some effort, he reaches inside, brings out a bundle of letters held together by a rubber band, and holds them out to me. "These are yours."

I look at the stack of letters in his hand, dozens of them piled up, sealed, and never sent, and I can't form a single word.

"I couldn't ever get it right," he says, "not like I wanted to, or like you deserved. Nothing I said ever matched up to the way I felt, and the way I felt was like I didn't deserve it. Like it was wrong that someone else had to die for me to live." He shrugs. "I didn't know how to say thank you for giving me life to someone who'd lost a person they loved. I couldn't, so I didn't. Just like you."

He holds out the bundle to me again. "These are your letters, as much as that other one was."

I look at them, and I can see the weight of his guilt, and of his heart, heavy with it. When I reach out, I know I'll never open a single one, but I also know he needs me to take them from him. So I do.

We sit there quiet in the dim light of his room, our secrets and scars laid out all around us. For a moment I wish we could go back to that magic place where we were together, free of our pasts. But I know we can't. We never really were free from them. As hard as we both tried, and as much as we both wanted it to be otherwise, we are made of our pasts, and our pains, our joys and our losses. It's in the very fibers of our beings. Written on our hearts.

The only thing we can do now is listen to what's in them.

I set the letters down on the table, and then I go to Colton. I ease myself onto his bed and lie down next to him. His puts his arm around me, and I rest my head on his chest. Listen to the steady rhythm that I want to keep hearing. "What now?" I ask.

"Now?" He laughs a little. "That's a big question." He pauses, and when I look up, I can see he's smiling. "I think we might have to answer that as we go," he says. "But right now . . ." He pulls me closer, kisses my forehead. "This is enough. This is everything."

"Thus, we say we 'learn by heart' that which we commit to memory or have understood thoroughly. And note, further, that the heart is believed to make possible a higher form of cognition, a level of understanding superior to that acquired by the brain."

—F. González Crussi, Carrying the Heart:
Exploring the Worlds within Us

CHAPTER THIRTY-FOUR

WE SIT FAR enough offshore to see the entire cove in the golden evening light. On one end, the waterfall spills over the cliff in slow motion, its currents rolling and tumbling all the way down to the sand, where they meet and mix with the waves that rush up the beach. On the other end is the set of stairs where I stood watching Colton in the water, unsure of how we could ever make sense together, but knowing that we did. That we do.

"This is the day I want, over and over," Colton says from behind me.

I turn to look at him. "Me too."

He smiles and shakes his head. "I can't believe you did this."

"I had some help from your sister." A lot of help, actually. When I called Shelby and told her what I wanted to do, she got it all set up for us: kayak, tent, campfire, s'mores, all of it.

"It's perfect," Colton says.

"Being cleared deserves a perfect day."

He smiles. "So does being the fastest new runner on the team."

It makes me laugh, but I really do feel good about it—so happy to have a plan, even if it's just to run, and take a few classes, and see where it goes.

"I don't know if that's *quite* up there with yours," I say, "but I'll take it, just like I'll take you coming with me."

"You should," Colton says with a smile.

He digs his paddle into the water, and we make our way onto the beach as the sunlight fades at our backs. After we rinse off in the waterfall, Colton lights the campfire and I watch the smoke curl up into the night, all the way to the stars. We roast marshmallows and talk about how many more perfect days we can spend together, about all the places we'll see and the things we'll do. All the possibilities for the future.

Later, when it starts to get cold, we pull our sleeping bags out of the tent and zip them together. Spread them out on the sand and lie there side by side, watching satellites and shooting stars cross the sky. I'm the best kind of tired from the sun and the ocean, but I don't want to close my eyes. I don't want this day to ever end, and I know Colton doesn't either by the way he keeps talking. Keeps telling me stories of the stars, and the sea.

He stops only to roll onto his side and pull me into him for a kiss. And in that kiss is one of those moments like we had in the hospital that day. A moment that is everything. It's a moment when I can feel the depth of the connection between Colton and me, between it all. I can feel the endless rhythms of light and dark, the tides and the winds. Life and death, and guilt and forgiveness.

And love. Always love.

We lie together, quiet, under an endless sky, beside a bottomless ocean, and we don't talk about how these are all the things that brought us together. We don't talk about how we wouldn't change any of them.

We don't have to, because these are the things we know by heart.

ACKNOWLEDGMENTS

FIRST AND ALWAYS, thank you to my husband, Schuyler, who had my heart the day we met and who is the reason I can write a love story in the first place.

Next, my deepest gratitude goes to Alexandra Cooper, who listened to and encouraged this idea when I first brought it up and who was there every step of the way after that with her gentle encouragement, sharp insights, and legendary (in the best possible way!) edit letters.

I do not have enough thank-yous for the indomitable Leigh Feldman, who saw me through this book from beginning to end as she does each time—with grace, humor, and a fierce heart.

So much gratitude for my new family at HarperCollins, who have made me feel welcome and taken care of from the very beginning. Rosemary Brosnan, Alyssa Miele, Renée Cafiero, Raymond Colón, Jenna Lisanti, and Olivia Russo—I am so deeply impressed by this dynamo team! And speaking of being impressed, I still look at this cover and marvel at the brilliance of Erin Fitzsimmons and her design that is so perfect for this story.

And then there are my dear friends who have become

my writing family. Sarah Ockler, who is my literary soul sister and who I feel lucky to know, and even luckier to call my friend. Here's to many more years of friendship, writing, wine, tarot, chocolate, and being amazing!

Morgan Matson, from the bunkhouse to our writing days at the library with Albino Bunny, you've been there for me as a friend and writing partner the whole way, and that means more to me than you could ever know. I look forward to many more years of writing with you, your smile, and your multiple beverages!

Carrie Harris, Elana Johnson, Stasia Kehoe, and Gretchen McNeil—you girls and your friendship, support, advice, hilarious emails, and general awesomeness have meant the world to me, and I can't picture doing this without you.

And finally, a friend who was a stranger until I stumbled on his story while doing research for this one: Zeke Kendall, who so patiently answered every last one of my questions so I could know all the little details, and whose story (and heart) is more amazing than anything I could ever write. (That's me calling you out, Zeke—time to write it!)